MAN BY THE POOL

MICHAEL HARTWIG

MAN BY THE POOL

Ebook ISBN: 979-8227974815
Printbook ISBN: 979-8218546724

First Edition October 2024
Second Edition November 2025

This is a work of fiction. Names, characters, businesses, places, events, locales, and incidents are either the products of the author's imagination or used in a fictitious way. Any resemblance to actual persons, living or dead, or actual events, is purely coincidental.

Special thanks to Flavia Vittucci, a Roman archaeologist and friend, who reviewed the manuscript and provided insights and feedback regarding Italian archaeological procedures and Italian expressions. Any inaccuracies are a result of the author's imagination and storytelling.

Cover Art by Author
Image is licensed from Shutterstock - Bill Perry - Ancient Roman Mosaic Baths Capitoline Museum Rome Italy

~ v

Contents

1

Chapter One – Angelo

A silky voice on Paolo's phone guided him through the narrow stone lanes of Frascati, a charming hill town just outside of Rome, famous for its crisp white wine. Paolo's head was pounding in the intense midday sun. He hadn't realized jet lag would be so pronounced and wished he had scheduled his meeting with Angelo for the day after his arrival. All he wanted to do was go to his hotel room, crank up the AC, and fall asleep.

"Ah, here it is," he murmured to himself, pressing the buzzer. He heard a lock click open in the antique wooden door and pushed it open, walking into an airy courtyard filled with bright red geraniums and a small fountain. He heard footsteps coming down a marble staircase to his right and glanced up.

"*Devi essere Paolo*," the man said warmly as he traversed the final two steps, introducing himself. "*Sono Angelo.*"

Paolo extended his hand to Angelo and said, "Paul. Paul Minetti."

"Nice to meet you, Paoul," he said, shifting from Paolo to Paul, raising his brows in surprise at the anglicizing of his name.

As was his habit, he scrutinized his new client carefully. From their correspondence, Angelo knew Paolo was forty-seven. He wasn't bad looking. He had a handsome face, but he wasn't in great shape. Paolo's light blue polo shirt showed no evidence of bulging biceps, defined pecs, or even broad shoulders. He seemed nervous or frustrated as beads of sweat formed on his forehead. His dark brown eyes darted back and forth, betraying his restlessness.

"Let's go upstairs to my office."

Paolo followed Angelo up the steep staircase into a spacious room. He breathed a sigh of relief as he felt cool air blowing from an air conditioner. "Have a seat," Angelo said, pointing to a comfortable leather chair. "Can I offer you some espresso, mineral water, wine?"

"Some water," Paolo replied. He glanced around the luminous room. Large windows faced breathtaking views of the surrounding countryside just outside the city center. Wood beams held up a vaulted ceiling, tall bookshelves lined the inside wall, and a rich, red Turkish carpet covered the brown tile floor.

Angelo opened a small refrigerator, pulled out a bottle of water, and poured them each a generous glass. Angelo sat at the large desk facing the center of the room. "So, how was your trip from Boston? You must be exhausted."

"Without incident. I'm a little tired, but glad to be here so that I can take care of things. The sooner the better." Paolo sat facing Angelo as if in an examination. Lawyers made him nervous and being in Italy added to his uneasiness. Angelo was roughly his parents' age. Angelo had known Paolo's grandfather and had come highly recommended as a real estate lawyer and notary, but he didn't make a good first impression. He was overweight, his clothes were wrinkled, and it appeared he was a heavy smoker, as an ashtray on his desk was filled with butts. In a disorganized frenzy, he rummaged through a mishmash of papers on his desk.

"Well, I'm glad to be of assistance. I want to go over a few things, and then we can go visit the property."

He glanced inside a file and pulled out an official-looking document. He continued, "The title to the land and house was in your grandfather's name. Through the fine work of the attorneys in Boston and here in Italy, the title is now registered in yours. I guess your power-of-attorney status worked in bypassing your parents' right to inherit the property. So, once we get an offer, it will be easy to complete the paperwork for a sale."

Paolo sighed and relaxed his shoulders. "Yes, my parents are in bad shape. It's good to hear the title is clear and there's no obstacle to unloading it."

"Are you sure you want to sell it?"

Paolo nodded. "I'm certain. There's nothing for me here," he said without equivocation. He stared emotionlessly at Angelo, tapping the side of his chair impatiently.

Angelo furrowed his forehead and cleared his throat. "It's a beautiful property, one most would give an arm and a leg for," he added, hoping to elicit some sentiment from his client. Paolo's grandfather, Carlo, was a larger-than-life kind of person. He loved Italy and the Roman countryside and would be horrified to know that his only grandson wanted to get rid of his little slice of heaven. Angelo wondered why Paolo seemed so disinterested in the property or in maintaining any connection with his heritage.

"Well, then, it shouldn't be difficult to sell. I want to get rid of it as quickly as possible." Paolo leaned forward in his chair.

"About that," Angelo said, raising a brow. "As I shared in several emails, the property has significant back taxes and bills that haven't been paid. Those have to be cleared up before you can put it on the market. Then there is the matter of the property itself. The plumbing and electricity are not up to code, and the house needs a lot of repairs. While some people may be willing to buy something and fix it up, you would have to sell the property at a very low price because of the defects. In my opinion, a quick renovation will be advantageous."

"I don't want to invest time or money. It's a headache, and I want to settle the estate as soon as I can. Let's just put it on the market. How much in back taxes and other bills do I owe?"

Angelo shuffled several folders on his desk and pulled one out of the stack. He glanced inside and shook his head. He leaned over the desk and showed Paolo the tax bill from the local municipality. "Here's the latest invoice, and that doesn't include utilities and other accounts."

"You're kidding!" Paolo exclaimed, his heart skipping a beat at the large sum. He knew his grandfather couldn't keep up with things at the end of his life, but he never imagined the magnitude he faced.

"I wish I were. I think it was during the bank debacle in 2008 that your grandfather started letting things slide. He had been selling parcels of the property to pay for taxes and upkeep. But after 2008, no one wanted to buy land. He was getting old. He must have been overwhelmed."

"What a fucking mess. I'll need the revenue from the sale of the property to cover all of this," Paolo said, wiping perspiration off his forehead.

"I'm afraid you'll have to get a short-term loan, then. That's why it makes sense to make repairs so that you know it will sell quickly and for a good price. You don't want to take out a loan to pay bills and then have things sit around because people are dissuaded by the work they would have to do."

"I don't have time for all of this," Paolo said angrily. He fidgeted in his chair and shook his head in frustration.

Angelo nervously sorted more papers and looked off into the distance, avoiding Paolo's agitated eyes.

Paolo stood abruptly. He began to pace back and forth, pressing his hand against his forehead. "Argh!" he exclaimed in frustration. "And what if I just walked away from it? I don't want it, and I can't imagine there will be much of a profit after paying taxes, bills, and repairs."

Looking up apprehensively at Paolo pacing back and forth, Angelo said, "You can't. No one will buy the property with the title in your name and unresolved financial issues."

"But the buyers could take care of those matters."

"They could, but most don't want to take on something like that. They imagine other problems that might be lurking under the surface and would be afraid to sign papers. And if no one buys it in the short-term, you are still liable for taxes and for any problems that might arise – such as accidents, squatters, or environmental problems."

"What a shitshow!"

"What about your father?"

"What about him?"

"Does he have funds to pay for things?"

Paolo glared at Angelo and then said, "He and my mother are ill. All of their savings are going to their medical care."

"I'm sorry."

"There must be some other option. I've got my own work to take care of back in Boston. I can't afford to waste a lot of time here."

"A crew is ready to begin work. They promised me they can fin-ish in two months. I assure you, once the repairs have been made and overdue bills paid, you won't have any trouble selling the land and the house."

"I've heard that before. Renovations always take longer than promised, and no one can guarantee real estate sales. It's a crap-shoot."

"I've been in the business for a long time. I know what I'm talking about. It will sell quickly."

"When could the crew begin?"

"The day after tomorrow."

Paolo looked quizzically at Angelo.

"Yes. I tentatively lined things up, knowing you were in a hurry."

"Well, thanks," Paolo said without much enthusiasm or warmth.

"I think you should see the property so you can appreciate what needs to be done. Shall we take a look?"

Paolo looked at his watch. "How long will it take? I'm tired and not in the mood to spend a lot of time looking at the house this afternoon."

"It's a short ride outside of town. It won't take long."

Paolo looked at his watch again and nodded reluctantly.

"I'll drive us. Are you ready?"

"Sure. Let's get this over with."

Angelo reached into his desk for the car keys and led Paolo down the stairs and out onto the street to his car.

"It's not a long drive. You must know the route."

"I haven't been here in a while."

Angelo gazed at Paolo incredulously.

"Your grandfather loved it here."

"Yes, he did. All he could talk about was Italy this and Italy that. I never understood why he didn't just move back here."

Angelo rolled his eyes. He shifted gears as he made several sharp turns on the winding road that led east of the city. The countryside was idyllic — vineyards clinging to the hillsides, cypress trees lining historic roads, groves of olive trees surrounding historic presses, and beautiful villas set on knolls with panoramic views of the surrounding landscape. Angelo glanced over and shook his head in disbelief as he noticed Paolo checking emails on his phone rather than enjoying the passing scenery.

Soon, Angelo turned down a gravel road. It was shaded by umbrella pines and lined with rows of unkempt grape vines. They pulled up to the front of the house, and Paolo quickly got out of the front seat and placed his hands on his hips as he studied the house. Angelo walked up behind him, placed a hand on his shoulder and said, "*Eccoci qua!*"

Paolo stared at Angelo as if to convey he didn't understand what he just said. He hated that people presumed he spoke Italian. His grandparents had spoken Italian to him since he was an infant, and he was fluent. But he detested the language and had no interest in using it.

Angelo gave him a curious look and repeated the phrase in English. "Here we are!"

Paolo took a few steps forward, gazing at the sight in front of him. "Shit," he said ponderously. The stone and plaster building had once been quite handsome — with a pitched terra cotta tile roof, wood-beamed eaves, and stone-framed windows. Frighteningly wide cracks had formed on the plaster façade, and broken terra cotta roof tiles were scattered in the dead bushes and overgrown grass in the front garden.

"As you can see, the house needs substantial work," Angelo noted.

"Are there foundation problems?" Paolo asked as he gazed at the building and shook his head in disbelief.

"We won't know until we get into the project."

"Is it better just to tear it down? Just sell the land?"

"Unfortunately, structures of this age are protected by historical regulations."

"I'm not believing this!" Paolo exclaimed with anger.

"Hmm, yes. I'm sorry."

"Let's see the rest of the place."

Angelo led him past what had once been a verdant herb and vegetable garden and was now a mishmash of toppled stone walls and weeds. A faded plaster statue of the Virgin Mary surprisingly remained upright on a cement pedestal. Paolo could almost imagine his grandmother picking herbs for sauce and clipping flowers for a vase she kept in the kitchen window. "The garden is an easy fix," Angelo noted as they traversed it on a narrow stone walkway. They continued forward, and Angelo added, "As you may recall, there is a spring-fed pool over there."

Paolo gazed down the hill toward a row of shade trees and spotted the dark green algae-filled basin. They walked toward it and pushed aside several rusty lounge chairs lining an old stone deck. "It's difficult to know what condition the pool is in. It needs to be emptied and cleaned."

Paolo felt his chest constrict. A flood of conflicting emotions coursed through him. The pool had been a refuge from his grandparents, a place where he escaped to recline in the sun, sip lemonade, listen to American music on his portable CD player, and close his eyes, hoping he would wake up back in Boston. It was also the setting of his first sexual fantasies, thoughts that haunted him still. He thought he had locked them all deep inside, but now, standing at the edge of the stagnant water, he was startled by how vivid and alive they were.

Angelo nudged him out of his daze and said, "Let's walk around the back and see the barn and cellar."

They traversed a walkway behind the house, where more tiles were missing from the roof and larger cracks had formed on the walls. About 50 meters from the house, they approached a structure built into the hillside.

"You must remember this combination barn and cellar where your grandfather kept his tractor and tools and made wine," Angelo noted as he searched for a key hidden behind some stones. He found it and opened the rusty lock, prying open the large antique wooden doors. He reached for a flashlight on a nearby shelf, turned it on, and beamed light into the cavernous space. "By the way, the electricity has been turned off. The work crew will have a generator. Once the electrician does his work, we can request that the utilities be restored. Come this way."

Angelo led Paolo into the cellar. It smelled of hay, oil, and earth. A faint aroma of fermented grapes floated through the air. On the left side of the entrance was an old tractor. Paolo believed it was the same vehicle he had driven nearly 30 years ago. He shook his head in disbelief.

Angelo pivoted to the other side of the space and gestured toward several tall stainless-steel vats. "Here is the equipment for making wine. From what I'm told, it is in relatively good shape."

They continued deeper into the cellar. Angelo continued, "These are the barrels your grandfather used to age the wine, and over there is what remains of his collection. The bottles are at least 10 years old."

"Do you think the wine is any good?" Paolo asked, trying to bring into focus the racks of bottles concealed by the shadows Angelo's flashlight created on the moist stone walls. Paolo feared they were intruding into the domain of mice and feral animals who, at any moment, might jump out and race past them.

"You'll have to try them."

Paolo raised his brows.

"What do you think?" Angelo asked, worried about Paolo's reaction.

"The cellar seems to be in relatively good shape, but let's go see the house. I have a feeling it's not going to be a pretty picture."

They retraced their steps and walked toward the back entrance of the villa. Angelo had a key and unlocked the weathered wooden door. They walked into the kitchen. There was a dead mouse on the plain tile floor near the refrigerator. Paolo opened its door and smelled the mold inside. "Shit!" he exclaimed.

He opened a couple of cabinets, discovering old cans of vegetables, jars of spices, and olive oil. "It's like everything is frozen in time," Paolo remarked.

"I imagine your grandparents thought they were coming back, and at some point, didn't. No one came afterwards to clear things out."

Paolo looked around the space and imagined the cost of replacing appliances, cabinetry, countertops, and flooring. He shook his head, fearing he was embarking on a terribly expensive renovation. They walked into the adjoining dining area, which was filled with an antique table, chest, and rickety chairs. Paolo ran his finger through the heavy layer of dust covering the oak surface. He could almost imagine his parents and grandparents gathered for a formal meal — passing pasta, salad, grilled vegetables, and crusty bread. Ambivalent feelings coursed through his chest — the proud sense of family and traditions mixed with regret at never being able to embrace them with enthusiasm.

"The place must bring back all kinds of fond memories," Angelo remarked as they slowly made their way to the center of the villa.

Paolo surveyed the living room and imperceptibly shook his head no. He hadn't been back to the house since he was a teenager. Over the years, he had come up with more and more clever excuses to avoid joining his family in the summers. As a child, he had been there often, but the memories weren't pleasant. Angelo's question was troubling.

Angelo added, "You will need to go through the place and decide what you want to keep and what to throw away before the workers come."

"Just throw it all away," Paolo said with little emotion.

Angelo raised his brows in surprise. "Are you sure? There may be mementos and valuable things that you want to hold on to or bring back to your parents."

"I don't think so."

"Well, I took the liberty of ordering a dumpster and a small storage container. They arrive early tomorrow. You can store what you want to keep and throw the rest away."

Paolo nodded, taking a quick inventory of the room.

"Is there anything else you want to show me? I think I've seen enough."

"There are the bedrooms and baths, but if you're ready to go, I can take you back to town. I'm sure it has been a tiring and stressful day."

"Thank you. I'm sorry I was so irritable earlier. I just didn't need this now. Between my parents' illnesses and my own work, I have enough on my plate. The quicker we can get rid of this, the better. I appreciate all you are doing."

"I liked your grandfather. Anything I can do for you is a way of honoring his memory."

"I guess everyone knew them," Paolo mused.

"Your grandparents were both well-liked. Everyone looked forward to their visits. It's a shame to see the place decline. With a little investment, it could be a showplace again. You could rent it out and use it from time to time yourself."

"I don't vacation in Italy, and I don't want the hassles or responsibilities of owning property here. I need to get rid of it."

"Suit yourself," Angelo said reluctantly.

Paolo felt a pinch in his chest. All his life, he resented the pressure his grandfather placed on him to learn Italian and to embrace his heritage. He dreaded becoming a *paisano* — using Italian gestures, celebrating Italian holidays, swapping recipes for sauce, marrying a good Italian girl, and passing on the same traditions to his kids. It felt so suffocating.

He knew he should feel relief that he could finally cut the cords to Italy and let go of the pressure he felt to live up to his grandparents' and parents' expectations. But he didn't. Rather, anger boiled inside. He resented that his grandparents had let things go and that the burden of taking care of the place – one he never liked in the first place - now fell on him. He was mad that his grandparents' lack of planning put him in such an untenable situation. It felt as if they were continuing to pressure him to cling to his culture, even from the grave. His chest tightened and his breathing strained as he pondered the task before him.

"If you don't mind, I'd like to go back to the hotel," Paolo said to Angelo, who had become distracted by an incoming text on his phone.

"Sure. Shall we?"

They got back into the car, and Angelo sped through the countryside toward Frascati. He dropped Paolo off in front of his hotel and returned to his office.

Once inside, Paolo called his parents. When his dad answered the phone, he said, "Dad, I made it to Frascati. Everything's fine. How are you doing?"

"We're good. Your sister is here checking on us."

"That's wonderful. How is she doing?" he asked, not having the heart to correct his dad. He didn't have a sister. It was the home health aide who was there taking care of them.

"Your sister is so helpful. She's made a delicious meal for us. Maybe we can all visit Italy next summer. You know how your mother loves the place," Paolo's father added.

"I'm sure that would be nice. Why don't you get some rest? I'll be back soon."

"Goodbye, son."

"Bye, dad."

Paolo fought tears that formed in his eyes. He didn't have the time or the luxury of being emotional. He had tasks to take care of, matters to settle, and work to do. Paolo hung up the phone and undressed. He slid under the fresh sheets and fell quickly asleep.

2

Chapter Two – Mementos

The next morning, Paolo stood immobile in the center of his grandparents' living room, overwhelmed by the task before him. All his life, he felt antipathy for the exaggerated affection his grandparents and parents had for Italy, for the vineyard, for the villa. The room seemed to mock him, filled with things that reminded him of them. He gazed at the cheap furniture unaesthetically arranged in the living room — a dusty sofa he remembered taking naps on and an overstuffed chair where his grandmother read her books. Religious statues rested on lace doilies, piles of old newspapers rested on the coffee table, and faded prints covered the walls.

He imagined relief at tossing the household items into the trash bin set in the middle of the room, finally erasing the past, expunging the sense of powerlessness and inadequacy he felt towards his family. He longed to cut cords and find his own way, unburdened by the expectations and script they kept waving in his face.

Paolo reached for a stack of books and newspapers and stared at them defiantly. He furtively glanced at the titles — all Italian romance novels. Rolling his eyes, he tossed them like basketballs into

the bin. He unfolded the newspapers and scanned the headlines —
another failed government, a banking crisis, and scandals involv-
ing politicians and movie stars. As he tossed them into the bin,
he noticed, at the last moment, an article on one front page about
the Pope encouraging more openness to gay people. He retrieved
the paper, read the report, and then tossed it back into the trash.
He wondered what his grandparents must have thought about the
Pope's overtures, and if they ever made the connection with their
grandson's sexuality.

Three framed photos on the mantel caught his attention. One
was of his grandparents' wedding, both of them dressed for the cer-
emony and leaning into each other. Carlo was exceedingly handsome, breathtakingly so. He had thick dark hair and deeply set
brown eyes. He gazed intensely at Luisa, with one of his brows
raised playfully. His grandfather had a kind of seductiveness to
him. He was always plotting, planning, cajoling, and it was difficult to resist him. People tried unsuccessfully to escape from being swept up in his vortex. Paolo had tried all his life to deflect
his grandfather's powerful influence and realized, even now, how
it goaded him.

Paolo's parents were in the other photo, tossing coins in the
Trevi fountain during their honeymoon. They were so young and
idealistic and excited about their life together. Rita had a warm
smile, betraying a thoughtful and generous spirit. Paolo could see a
little of his grandfather in Enzo, the playfulness of his eyes and the
sparkle in his smile.

The third photo was of the four of them holding Paolo just before his baptism. Paolo took hold of the photo and scrutinized it
carefully. It was difficult to imagine his parents and his grandparents so young and full of life. They were happy, smiling excitedly
at little Paolo. Paolo detected the enthusiasm and the dreams that

must have been swirling in their heads as they looked at their son, their grandson, at the one who would carry on the family.

Paolo took a deep breath and raised his brows as he gazed at the statue of the Holy Family placed strategically amongst the photos. He had been told repeatedly that it was blessed by the Pope and had special powers. He took the photos and statue and placed them face down in the cardboard box Angelo had delivered to the house earlier in the morning, one that would hold fragile mementos to be preserved.

He pivoted and reached for the reproduction prints on the walls — classics by Da Vinci, Michelangelo, Raphael, and Caravaggio. They were faded and cheaply framed. He tossed them into the trash bin. He carried the rickety chairs and side tables outside to the dumpster and heaved them over the rim. They crashed like dead carcasses on the bare metal bottom of the container.

Back inside, he walked down the hallway to the bedrooms. He feared that at any moment his grandfather or grandmother might appear around a corner, give him an enthusiastic embrace, and sit him down for a heart-to-heart talk. He smelled the stale odor of the cigarettes they smoked, the cheap fragrance they spritzed on their collars, and the distinctive smells that clung to Carlo's work clothes — fertilizer, dung, and grape must.

Cautiously, he pressed open the door to their room. The shades were closed, and the room was stuffy and warm. He opened the shutters and pivoted, scrutinizing the expansive space. Perhaps the only piece of furniture worth keeping in the house was the antique bed with a decorative carved oak headboard. A dusty quilt, one Luisa had brought from Boston to Italy, rested on top of the old, curved mattress. A few decorative pillows added some color and charm to the room.

Paolo approached their closet with apprehension, fearing how he might react when he saw his grandmother's dresses or his grandfather's jackets and suits. In his mind, he knew Carlo and Luisa weren't there. The garments had clothed them, but they weren't them. He took a deep breath as he ran his hand over his grandmother's dresses – the bright floral prints she was so fond of and wore so well while she entertained guests. Paolo leaned over and sniffed the dark blue jacket his grandfather wore to the city and to church and detected the lingering scent of his cologne.

He thought he had moved on since their deaths and had made peace with the regrets that gnawed at his gut. It had been difficult to overlook the disappointment and sadness on their faces as they whispered their farewells to him — first Carlo and a few months later, Luisa. He hadn't married or produced a great-grandson for them, and they sensed Paolo's underlying disdain for them in his feeble attempts to express affection and love as they faded and passed on.

Paolo gathered the clothes and carried them to the living room, where he tossed them into the trash bin. A master at suppressing emotions, Paolo wasn't sure if he felt liberation, sadness, or anger — or perhaps a little of each. He glared into the bin for a moment and then pivoted, walking down the hallway to the other bedrooms.

Inside the dresser of a room that had served as an overflow storage area, Paolo discovered a shoebox filled with photos. He opened the lid and peered inside. Several Polaroid snapshots rested on top of a pile of pictures — old sepia prints, a few black and white images, and some faded color photos. While curious, he didn't feel like he had the luxury or time to go through them. He unceremoniously took them into the living room and included them with other items to keep.

A car approached the house, a cloud of dust trailing behind it. The glare on the windshield was too strong for him to identify the driver. A woman stepped out of the vehicle, someone roughly his age. She wore short shorts and a loose, low-cut white blouse that showcased her ample bosom, gleaming in the sun. She walked toward the front porch, and Paolo stepped outside.

"*Buongiorno*," the woman said. "*Sono Joanna.*"

"Paul Minetti. How can I help you?"

"*Sono la nipote di Aurora, la sorella della tua nonna.*"

Although Paolo understood Joanna's introduction, he furrowed his brow as if he didn't understand.

"I'm Joanna," she repeated in English. "Your grandmother's great-niece."

Luisa didn't speak often of her family, so Paolo couldn't place Aurora or Joanna. "Ah. So how can I help you?"

"I understand your grandparents have passed, and I came to see if you needed any help. I brought some cheese and wine in case you were hungry," she said as she held up a sack.

"That's kind of you, but I am fine."

Joanna glanced around and remarked, "Looks like quite the project. Are you renovating the house?"

"Selling it."

"I didn't realize," she said disingenuously. She had heard through a lawyer friend about the transfer of title and rumors of its future sale.

"Yes, I'm afraid we have to let it go. My parents are ill, and I have no interest in keeping it."

She shook her head. "It's such a special place."

Paolo stared at her without emotion.

"Let me help you. It looks like a lot of work for one person."

"There are workers coming tomorrow. I'm all set."

"Okay, but do you mind if I take a look? It's been a while since I last visited," Joanna persisted.

Paolo extended his arm and gestured to her. "Be my guest. I'm sure you must know your way around."

Joanna nodded, although she had only seen the place when she was a teenager. Her grandmother and Paolo's grandmother had become estranged. She wasn't certain of the details. Passing in front of Paolo, Joanna could feel the intensity of his gaze.

Paolo followed her as she meandered through the empty living room toward the dining room and kitchen.

A large oak table took up most of the space adjacent to the kitchen. An antique glass hutch filled with plates and glasses lined one wall, and a large painting of the Holy Family hung on the other side of the room. Joanna walked up to it and peered closely. "This is impressive!"

Paolo had never really paid much attention to it. He approached Joanna from behind and observed her run her fingers over the surface. "It's an original."

Paolo furrowed his brows and touched the surface. "Do you know the artist?"

Joanna wasn't much into art history and had no idea who the painter was. "No. But whoever it is, he or she was quite talented. Look at the colors!"

"Hmm," Paolo murmured, stepping back to get a feel for the composition. "My grandfather had a devotion to images of the Holy Family."

"What will you do with this?"

Originally, Paolo had planned to toss it into the trash, like everything else. Now he began to reconsider. Maybe it was worth something. "Not sure," he said. He took hold of the frame. He took it off the picture hook and turned it around, noticing an inscription. "*Una copia della Sacra Familia di Andrea del Sarto. Lorenzo Castelli. 1990. Per Carlo e Luisa, con affetto.*"

Paolo showed the writing to Joanna. She translated it for him, said, "Looks like it was an original copy done for your grandparents in 1990. A copy of a piece by Andrea del Sarto."

"Hmm," Paolo murmured, pretending to be surprised. What actually surprised him was that the painting would have been in the house when he last visited in 1995, and he didn't recall it. He set it carefully against the wall, glancing back at it as he led Joanna toward the kitchen.

"You must remember this space," he added.

She smiled and nodded, trying to contain her disgust at the dead roaches spread across the counter. "Let me get a cloth and a trash bag and help you clean this," she offered.

"Be my guest," Paolo replied, realizing her help might be a blessing after all.

Joanna pulled a few drawers open and found some kitchen towels. She found a trash bag under the sink and opened the cabinets, tossing old boxes and jars into it. "This is disgusting," she remarked, using a small hand brush to slide the debris into the bag. She opened the refrigerator and shouted, "*Cazzo!*"

From the other side of the house, Paolo grinned as he imagined Joanna peering into the moldy refrigerator. He decided to take advantage of the cooler morning air and tackle projects outside, clearing weeds, gathering broken roof tiles, and tossing ruined outdoor furniture into the dumpster.

An hour later, Joanna came outside with two cups of espresso. "*Ecco,*" she said as she handed him one.

Paolo looked at her incredulously and inquired, "How did you make coffee?"

"I brought some ground coffee, and the gas stove still works."

"The kitchen must have been disgusting."

"It was. But not anymore."

"Thank you," he said reluctantly.

They stood in the shade of one of the pine trees and sipped the espresso. Joanna asked, "You don't remember me, do you?"

Paolo shook his head no.

"It was one of the summers you spent here. I think we were both seventeen."

"Ah. That was a long time ago."

"Hmm, yes."

"Did you see my grandparents and parents often when they visited?"

"Actually, no. There was a falling out."

"Over what?"

"I'm not sure. Some history with your grandfather."

"Any specifics?"

"Afraid not. I just recall that my grandmother knew your grandparents were here and fretted that she hadn't been invited for a visit. But I never knew the background."

"And you? Do you have a family?"

Joanna chuckled. "No. I'm the youngest. It's my job to take care of the old ones. First my grandparents and then my parents."

Paolo gave her an odd look.

"I know. It's an old Italian custom that should be changed. But we're still rather traditional."

Paolo thought of his own parents back in Boston and felt a pinch in his chest.

Joanna then added, "And you?"

"Hmm," Paolo began with a murmur. "If you mean, am I married, no."

"Taking care of your parents?"

"Yes. But I'm an only child."

"Ah, then, that's worse. You are expected to carry on the family line as well as take care of everyone."

Paolo pondered Joanna's words and realized that after years of therapy, the pressure he felt had never been so clearly stated. He looked at her without emotion.

She asked, "Your profession?"

"Investment broker."

She smiled. Paolo worried that she thought he was rich.

"You?"

"*Dolce far niente.*"

Paolo knew the expression, the Italian art of sweetly doing nothing. He looked at her quizzically.

"I've perfected the art of leisure."

"I'm sure that's not the case if you are taking care of your family."

"*Beh.* They're in relatively good shape at the moment."

"Well. I guess I should continue cleaning up. Don't feel like you have to stay," Paolo said.

"It's nothing. I brought wine, cheese, and bread for later. I can help clean out the inside if you want to tackle things out here."

Paolo didn't like Joanna hanging around. He wanted solitude. He nervously watched a drop of sweat run down her neck and into the folds of her bosom. "It's quite alright. I can take care of things myself. It's a hot day. No need for you to hang around."

"I have nothing else to do."

Shit, Paolo thought in his head. It was going to be difficult to shake her. He'd have to be more creative. "Whatever."

Paolo stood and walked toward the pool. Joanna remained in place and followed him with her eyes. She yelled as he got closer to the dark green watery mass. "That's going to be quite a project. Let me fetch some supplies — brushes, chlorine, and a pump."

"There's no electricity," Paolo shouted back, hopeful he had found a way to deter her.

"We have a generator at home. I'll be right back."

Paolo glanced at Joanna, who jumped into her car and sped off down the gravel road. It felt like his teenage years all over again — the blurred boundaries and suffocating familiarity that seemed part of Italian culture. He felt his skin become clammy.

In a short while, Joanna returned. She opened the hatch of her car and began to unload things. Paolo walked toward the car. "Wow! Looks like you brought half the hardware store."

"It's not that much. Hopefully, the spring is still working, and we can fill it up after we clean it out."

They carried equipment to the side of the pool. "First order of business is to pump out this shit," Joanna said matter-of-factly, scrunching her nose in disgust at the stagnant mass in front of them.

"Let me help you," Paolo said as he glanced over the equipment and tried to figure out what was what. He was more knowledgeable of machines and tools than most gay men, as his grandfather was a plumber and Paolo used to help him from time to time. He carried the generator and the pump to the pool deck, attached a long tube to the pump, and lowered it into the pool.

"You might want to add this," Joanna said, as she held up a protective net cover. "You never know what's down there. You don't want to suck up a dead animal into the pump."

Paolo looked into the dark green abyss; his eyes widened in horror. He pulled out the tube, affixed the strainer, and lowered it back down. Meanwhile, Joanna had connected the pump to the generator and turned it on. She flipped a valve, and soon dark green water began to spew out of the pump into a ravine below the pool.

They both stood over the edge and watched the water line slowly recede. Both were curious as to what they would uncover. "It might take a while," Joanna remarked. "Want something to eat?"

Paolo nodded, continuing to stare at the pool.

Joanna went back to the house and brought out wine, cheese, and bread. "It's simple, but it will do the job."

"Thanks," Paolo remarked with little warmth or enthusiasm.

They ate in the shade of a large pine tree while the pump hummed in the background.

"How does the pool work?" Paolo asked between bites of Asiago cheese Joanna had cut into small chunks. "It's been ages since I helped my grandfather."

"The spring fills the pool. When it reaches a certain level, the water goes into the overflow and into a drain."

"Do we have to treat the water?"

Joanna nodded as she took a sip of wine. She broke off a bit of crusty Italian bread and pressed it against some Gorgonzola cheese and put it in her mouth. When she finished, she added, "There should be a pump and filter someplace. It will need replacing. And you will need to add chlorine."

"Ah," Paolo remarked, calculating the added costs.

"So, your parents are not doing well?"

Paolo nodded no. "My father has Alzheimer's, and my mother has heart issues."

"Sorry to hear. You must have your plate full taking care of them."

"That's why I need to sell the vineyard."

Joanna glanced off and then turned to Paolo. "I don't know how to put this, but if they weren't around, would you keep it?" Joanna looked tenderly into Paolo's eyes.

He felt the intensity of her regard. He knew more was implied in her question than curiosity about the fate of the villa. While Paolo found the notion of a romantic relationship with a second cousin unsettling, the idea of a sex with Joanna was even more troubling. Over the years, Paolo's grandfather had paraded dozens of women before him, and out of some sense of obligation, he had tried as hard as he could to imagine relationships with them. Joanna wasn't unappealing — she had silky brunette hair, expressive eyes, a nice figure, and abundant breasts. She was friendly, warm, and jovial. But as he gazed at her, he arrived at the same visceral reaction he had with all women when he tried to visualize having sex. He couldn't imagine being able to do it.

"No. My life is in Boston."

"Beyond your parents, do you have other family there?"

Paolo nodded no and plopped another piece of cheese in his mouth. He realized he had more family connections in Italy than in Boston, but in Boston he didn't have to face the scrutiny of extended family and the expectation of embracing their traditions.

Joanna raised a brow. She found it hard to fathom Paolo's isolation from his roots. She took a long sip of wine and looked over at the pool, where the tube in the pool began to gurgle. She stood, and Paolo followed. They leaned over the edge.

"Surprisingly free of debris," Joanna remarked.

"Hmm," Paolo murmured. "Yes. Now what?"

Joanna reached for a container of chlorine powder and sprinkled it around the walls and on the bottom of the basin. "We can let this eat at the algae for a while, and then we can brush things down. Let's go look at the spring and see what's up. I don't see any water coming in."

They followed the incline of the hill above the pool. About twenty meters into a grove of trees, they found a spring gurgling up out of the ground. It was clear and cold. Nearby was an old plastic pipe that had been detached from the feed pipe for the pool. They reconnected it. Water soon began to splash into the cement pool.

Both looked at each other and smiled, walking briskly back. "Let me see if I can find some work clothes in the house," Paolo suggested.

Joanna nodded and glanced down at herself. "I'm all set." She stepped into the shallow end with a broom and began to brush the surface. The chlorine worked like a charm. The green algae came free from the surface and slid toward the drain.

Paolo returned wearing an old pair of shorts and a tee shirt he found in one of the dressers and eased himself down into the pool, using another brush to work the sides. They brushed and scraped the walls and then rinsed the slime off with buckets of spring water.

After a couple of hours, the pool was clean. They opened the spigot and allowed the fresh water to fill the basin. "Another glass of wine?" Joanna inquired as she sat on a stone wall near the pool deck.

"No thanks. I have more to do inside." He hoped she might leave.

"Take a break. It's hot, and you've accomplished a lot already."

"No. I have to get things ready for the crew tomorrow."

"I'm sure they can handle whatever's left. Sit. Relax. You're in Italy."

That's precisely what Paolo hated hearing. He had things to do — not the least of which included logging into his office and taking care of some transactions. He never figured out how Italy functioned. No one seemed to work. Everyone was either sitting in cafes or strolling about aimlessly.

"No. I have to finish a few things here and then do some work on my computer."

Joanna looked disappointed. Paolo knew he should be more grateful and sociable, but all he wanted was for her to leave so he could be alone. He stared back at her without expression.

She stood and began to gather her tools and equipment in a huff. Paolo picked up the generator and accompanied her to the car. "Thanks for your assistance," he said.

"Well. If you need any more help this week, let me know," she said, turning sideways to nod goodbye. She batted her luscious eyes as she extended her bosom forward, hoping she might elicit second thoughts. As she lowered herself into the driver's seat, she leaned out of the door and said, "Or if you want to get something to eat in town, call me. Here's my number," she said, handing him a card with her contact information.

Joanna sped off. She looked in her rearview mirror and shook her head. "Insolent son of a bitch. He hasn't changed a bit," she murmured to herself. She reached over to the console and turned on some music, hoping to drown out the thoughts racing through her head. Why was Paolo so aloof? Why hadn't he been back to Italy in all these years? And why did he have to be so damn handsome?

Paolo glanced at the dust trailing Joanna's car and rolled his eyes. Joanna's visit had brought back vivid and painful memories — the summer from hell, as he often referred to it. He vaguely remembered her and the entourage of cousins and their friends gathered around the pool all afternoon — taking in the sun, sipping drinks, and making small talk in Italian. His grandparents had placed great pressure on him to entertain the young people – providing food and drink. Luisa was busy all day making appetizers, and Carlo preened here and there on his tractor or in the garden, scrutinizing his grandson carefully and orchestrating social opportunities.

Paolo looked over at the pool, the source of so many conflicting emotions. He was glad they had cleaned it, but it mocked him still. He pivoted quickly, avoiding a protracted glance. He returned to the house, gathered up a few things, and returned to his hotel in town.

3

Chapter Three – The Crew

The next day, as Paolo rode up the long driveway, he noticed several commercial vehicles parked in front of the house. He pulled up near the cellar, stepped out of the car, and walked toward the group of men talking among themselves. They looked up as he approached.

"*Buongiorno. Sono Edoardo,*" one said as he extended his hand to Paolo. Edoardo was a short, muscular man with a warm smile and playful eyes.

"Paul, Paul Minetti," Paolo responded, giving Edoardo and his colleagues a quizzical look.

"We are workers. From Angelo," Edoardo said in broken English. "*Gino, Lorenzo, Piero, e Giovanni,*" he said, introducing his coworkers.

Paolo nodded awkwardly. He scrutinized them carefully.

"Make house *bella,*" Edoardo said enthusiastically, glancing toward the house.

Paolo furrowed his brow. "Not *bella.* Just fix."

Edoardo frowned.

"Sell house," Edoardo said as both a statement and a question. "Money."

"I don't want to spend a lot of money," Paolo said unequivocally.

"Spend money. Make money," Edoardo emphasized.

Paolo nodded no. He didn't want to spend money to make money. He began to perspire, sensing he was walking into a money trap. He looked at the crew and asked, "English?"

They nodded no. Gino held up his hand and pressed two fingers together. "A little."

Paolo raised his voice, as if volume would compensate for vocabulary. He spoke slowly. "I . . . don't . . . want . . . to . . . spend . . . a . . . lot . . . of . . . money. Just repair. *Riparare non rinnovare*," Paolo concluded in a few Italian words.

The crew nodded to each other as if they understood.

Edoardo ordered his colleagues. "To work!" They picked up their tools and headed to the house. Fearing they would begin to demolish things to the point that more expensive repairs would be necessary, Paolo felt a heavy pit in his stomach. He shadowed Edoardo, who, with each crew member, pointed out things needing attention.

Piero was the roofer, and Edoardo pointed to the broken tiles needing repair. Giovanni stood near them. At some point, Edoardo turned to him and began pointing to the large cracks in the façade and the gaps between the windows and the stone window frames that would need repair. Giovanni shook his head and mumbled some words to Edoardo. Paolo heard the words — *molto male, fondazione, pavimento* - and realized the cracks in the façade indicated more serious foundation issues that might require significant repairs and new flooring.

Paolo followed Edoardo inside the house. He found the fuse box and began to run his fingers over the antiquated electrical system. He gave Paolo a look and said, "We make new."

Paolo feared what that would cost him. He only replied, "Inexpensively."

Edoardo said, "*Ci proveremo.* We will try."

Paolo said, "Thanks. Important."

"Spend money. Make money," Edoardo insisted.

"I don't have much money," Paolo underscored, glaring at Edoardo.

Edoardo began to pull fuses out of the box and examined wires that led from the box toward various sections of the house. He gave Paolo a look, and Paolo realized Edoardo wanted him to vanish.

Paolo walked outside toward the cellar. He figured it might be a nice project to tackle while the workers focused on the house. He retrieved the key and unlocked the large wooden doors, letting light into the barn-like space. Carlo's old tractor caught his attention right away, and he approached it. It was a vintage machine Carlo used for cutting weeds between rows of vines and breaking up the soil in the spring to soak up rain. It was dusty and covered in hardened mud.

Paolo sat on the driver's seat and scrutinized the controls. Surprisingly, the ignition key was in place. Paolo turned it, but he heard only a click. The battery had to be dead, and he wondered if there was any fuel in the tank. He went back to the house, went inside, and found Edoardo.

"Tractor. Battery. Diesel."

Edoardo nodded as if he understood and went out of the back door to find Gino.

They both returned, and Gino said, "*Vi porto.* I bring you." He waved him forward.

"Battery," Gino said, looking toward the cellar.

Paolo nodded, went inside, and returned with the dead battery. Gino signaled for Paolo to get into his truck, and they sped off down the driveway and out onto the roadway.

At first, there was an awkward silence in the cab of Gino's truck — a period of adjusting to their proximity while not really knowing each other.

"*Lei è Americano?*" Gino asked, trying to start some conversation.

Paolo understood Gino's interest in confirming that he was American, but didn't want to give away that he understood Italian. He just nodded affirmatively.

Out of the corner of his eye, he checked out Gino, who was young — perhaps nineteen or twenty — and cute. Gino's muscular legs were dark and hairy. He had a closely cropped dark beard and a beautiful head of hair, shortly trimmed on the side, with thick, playful curls on the top.

Gino pointed up ahead and said proudly, "Fifteen minutes. Station. Diesel."

Although dressed in work clothes, Gino had applied a spritz of cologne earlier in the day — one with an intoxicating scent. He glanced over at Paolo from time to time with a seductive and playful smile. Encouraged by Gino's warmth, Paolo found himself undressing him with his eyes — first his pullover, then his shorts, then his briefs. He wondered what Gino looked like aroused and whether his friendliness was a sign of an affinity of sorts, whether he might be gay, too. He wondered if attitudes about gay people in Italy were more conservative, traditional, and repressive. If Gino wasn't gay, could he detect Paolo's roving eye, his curiosity, his desires? Paolo chuckled at himself — at his shameless fantasies and the inappropriateness of it all, particularly with someone so much younger. Hoping to deflect attention from any vibes he might be giving off, Paolo asked, "Plumber?"

"*Si*," Gino said proudly. "*Mio padre. Mio nonno.* My father. My grandfather," he clarified with a thick accent.

"Ah," Paolo noted without elaboration, realizing how pervasive family trades must be in Italian culture.

Gino glanced over at Paolo to engage him in conversation but noticed Paolo peering at his legs. Surprised, he raised a brow. He mumbled a few words in Italian, and Paolo pretended not to understand. Gino reached for the radio and turned on some music to fill the awkward silence.

Soon they arrived at a small gas station and garage surrounded by old metal storage structures. The owner recognized Gino and smiled. Several workers glanced up and observed the American. Paolo felt conspicuous, realizing they probably didn't see many foreigners in such a rural area.

Gino explained they needed a battery and some fuel. The owner went inside the shop and returned with a new battery and a container. He went to the pump and filled the canister, staring intensely at Paolo but saying nothing. When it was full, he noted the amount of fuel, the price, and scribbled a figure on some paper, handing it to Paolo.

Paolo nodded and asked, "Credit card?" as he pulled a card out of his wallet. The man nodded and gestured for Paolo to follow him. Inside, they processed the sale. Paolo and Gino got back into the truck. Gino waved to the owner and winked. The owner glanced intensely toward Paolo, who felt increasingly uncomfortable and out of place.

Inside the truck, Gino pulled out his phone and pushed a button, connecting with someone on the other end. They began to visit in local dialect. Paolo listened carefully and picked up a few words — *Americano, frocio, bello.* Gino glanced over at him from time to time, and Paolo pretended not to understand or register what he was saying. He concluded Gino had somehow figured out that he was gay — or at least there was a good chance he was — and was in the process of describing him to a friend. He was relieved that at least Gino thought was handsome, having used the word *bello.*

When they arrived, Paolo nodded to him and said, "*Grazie.*" He felt Gino's eyes linger before he returned to his colleagues.

Paolo walked to the cellar, attached the battery, and filled the tank with fuel. He cranked the ignition, and to his surprise, heard a few tentative pops. Suddenly, the engine began to run. He pressed in the clutch, shifted the gears, and slowly drove the tractor outside the barn and toward the field. The crew all gazed in amazement as Paolo guided the tractor along the gravel road.

When Paolo got to the first row of vines, he lowered the cutting device and heard the whirling noise of blades spinning. He drove between the rows and watched as the machine cleared a wide swath through the overgrowth.

The smell of freshly cut grass and broken earth filled the air. Paolo found it primitive, elemental, soothing. His life back home was cerebral — days filled with numbers, charts, and transactions. There was an odd satisfaction that overcame him as he made his way through the field — not having to think, just being in the midst of nature and accomplishing a simple repetitive task. He didn't mind the sweat forming on his body or the bounce of the tractor as it traversed the uneven earth.

His grandfather's vineyard had been larger when Paolo was younger. Over the years, as Carlo sold off parcels, it became more modest. Old wire and posts separated Carlo's land from his neighbor's. After Paolo finished mowing between the vines, he noticed a few areas needing repair. He returned to the cellar, retrieved some pliers and hammers, and made the fixes.

Walking back to the cellar, he observed the vines. They were bright green and leafy. Buds had formed on the branches, buds that would eventually become the grapes the region was famous for. Locals cultivated the fields as far back as the fifth century BCE. Paolo's grandfather grew three types of grapes — Malvasia, Greco Bianco, and Trebbiano — all typical of the region.

Paolo's grandfather had laboriously tutored Paolo in grape cultivation when he was younger. He knew the vines were overgrown. They needed to be trimmed to ensure that the fruit would be robust. Paolo shook his head, realizing how much work there was to do. Well-tended vines would fetch a better price when he put the house on the market. He glanced at the workers and wondered if they might have cousins who could tend the fields.

Paolo grew hungry and returned to town to change clothes and get something to eat. When he returned, the crew was still busy at work. Edoardo had pulled wires as a prelude to rewiring the home. Gino had already dug a trench to locate the source of water and to check the condition of the pipes. Piero was on the roof, taking an inventory of tiles and marking areas for repairs, and Lorenzo and Giovanni were already mixing cement to fill major cracks in the façade of the structure.

At three in the afternoon, the crew began to tire. Edoardo approached Paolo, who was clearing the herb and vegetable garden. "We finish for today. Swim?" he asked, glancing at the pool.

Paolo nodded.

Edoardo yelled to his crew that they could stop work. They wrapped up their tools and equipment and began to make their way to the water. Paolo observed from a distance, concealing himself behind a bush at the edge of the garden. The men stripped and leaped in, splashing each other playfully.

Out of the group of workers, Gino caught Paolo's attention. Seeing him in the flesh, he realized his earlier whims were well-founded. Gino had a slim frame, caramel skin, a light coating of dark hair on his chest, and was well endowed, his cock bouncing up and down as he played with the others. Gino had a mischievous smile and dark eyes.

At one point, Gino pulled himself out of the pool to recline on the adjacent rocky terrace so that the sun would dry him. Paolo scrutinized him from afar. Gino's wet torso glistened in the light, his chest rising and falling with each breath. Gino adjusted his cock, seemingly proud of its size.

Paolo had no difficulty recreating the image of another young man he had observed at the same pool, someone who looked very much like Gino. It was thirty years ago.

Mauro was seventeen. He wore a red Speedo, one that complemented his dark olive complexion. As Mauro sunned, his firm cock pressed against the wet fabric of his suit, leaving little to the imagination. Behind his dark sunglasses, Mauro seemed aloof and inscrutable. A coterie of teenage girls Paolo's grandfather had invited, sipped lemonade, giggled, and paraded back and forth on the pool deck, trying to get Mauro's attention.

The young girls had already concluded that Paolo was *antipatico*. He heard them murmur the word often. He was unfriendly, and they concluded he was spoiled and self-absorbed. They paid him little regard.

Mauro, on the other hand, seemed to relish their attention and knew just the right words and expressions to keep them interested, to keep them hovering nearby. He hid behind his dark glasses, but that only encouraged them to flirt more and find creative ways to engage him.

Paolo rolled his eyes at the games they played. He found it difficult to believe that someone as handsome as Mauro could be so gullible and fall for their shallow antics. He imagined Mauro to be intelligent and clever. His noble features suggested refinement, education, and discriminating taste. Paolo secretly hoped there might be an affinity between them, and longed for a glance of recognition, some sign that Mauro saw past the surface, felt their kinship, even if he had to pretend indifference.

As Paolo observed the pool and the workers splashing about, he spotted a grove of bushes up the hill. It was there that the betrayal took place, one that marked a terrible turning point. His grandmother, Luisa, had just served lemonade and cookies. All the young people had gathered around a table to consume the goodies. Diana, one of the neighborhood busybodies, took advantage of the distraction. With her abundant breasts straining the tight fabric of her bikini, she took Mauro's hand and led him up the hill. Paolo watched from behind his dark glasses as they ducked behind several laurel bushes, invisible to everyone but him.

Paolo had not been surprised by Diana's voracious lips on Mauro's mouth, nor her nimble hands running through his thick black hair. He was unprepared, however, when he noticed Diana slip her hands inside the back of Mauro's swimsuit and massage his buttocks, firm and round.

The subsequent exchange was quick and transactional — at least Paolo hoped it had been devoid of any sentiment on Mauro's part. But the image of Mauro's buttocks squeezing and flexing in the bright midday Italian sun as they consumed their lust left a lasting impression. How could Mauro change sides? How could he betray their unspoken but undeniable bond — one not of blood but of some kind of aesthetic sensitivity? Surely Mauro wouldn't succumb to the manipulative flirts of the girls or be seduced by tits, curvy hips, batting eyes, or, God forbid, a vagina.

As Paolo recreated the scene in his head, he realized that at seventeen, he didn't have a name for the team he believed he and Mauro were members of. No mascot had been chosen, no captain voted in, or squad composed. All Paolo knew was that Mauro had betrayed their unnamed tribe and left him adrift in an alien world. Paolo gave one more scrutinizing look at Gino stretched out in the sun and shook his head — an appetizing bit of eye candy in a world Paolo had fought hard to dislike and disdain. He resolved to pre-serve the shell he had erected many years ago, sell the farm, and return to Boston. Nothing would melt his resolve!

4

Chapter Four – The Discovery

Paolo had a restless night, tossing and turning as thoughts raced through his head. The house renovation weighed heavily on him, and the memories of Mauro haunted him. Early in the morning, he stumbled out of bed, dressed, and headed to the nearby cafe for coffee and a croissant.

The ever-present sound of Italian floated beside him as he walked down the street and entered the small establishment. Growing up, he was surrounded by his grandparents' native language. It was like a constant background noise, one he tried to tune out but never quite could.

Women and men chatted as they pressed against the bar, sipping cappuccinos, and breaking off pieces of flaky croissants, plopping them into their mouths. Local cafes were the epicenter of neighborhoods, the place where people connected and shared news. Paolo observed them speaking with their hands and eyes. He knew the gestures and the implications and chuckled, recalling his parents and grandparents carrying on whole conversations similarly.

In English, Paolo ordered a double espresso and a cream-filled croissant. Espresso was one of the few things Italian that Paolo had embraced with enthusiasm. He loved the frothy caramel foam floating over the dark liquid and the rich flavor of Italian roast.

Just outside the café, old men gathered around small tables, reading newspapers, and discussing soccer, politics, money, and beautiful women. One looked just like his grandfather and deflated whatever remained of Paolo's flimsy attempt to erase the memories of his past. Another at the table yelled to Paolo, "*Giovanotto. Sei il nipote di Carlo Minetti?*"

Paolo shook his head, pretending he didn't understand. He finished the espresso in a quick gulp, wrapped his croissant in a napkin, and walked briskly away. The locals could see the resemblance and were certain Paolo was Carlo's grandson. Paolo wanted to disappear.

He retrieved his car and drove to the villa, parking near the cellar. Edoardo and his crew were busy at work and nodded to him as he got out of the car. He opened the cellar doors so that the bright sunlight filled the space. Edoardo walked toward him.

"*Buongiorno,*" Edoardo began.

"Hello," Paolo replied. "How are the renovations coming?"

"*Molto lavoro.* Follow. Questions," he said as he waved Paolo toward the house.

Inside the kitchen area, Edoardo began to describe what they had discovered and what they needed his authorization for. "Plumbing and electricity need work but no *grande problema.*" Paolo sighed with relief.

Paolo followed Edoardo's hand as he pointed to the sink, faucet, and lights and implied no need for alterations, just replacements and a few upgrades. He caught the gist and nodded.

Edoardo pointed to various cabinets in the room. "Remove these. Put shelves. Paint these."

Paolo nodded and smiled approvingly. The idea of open shelving in part of the kitchen seemed like a nice and stylish alternative to buying new cabinets.

Edoardo waved him toward the bedrooms and baths.

"Same?" he asked, wondering if Paolo wanted any changes to the layout of the house.

Paolo nodded. "Keep the same."

Edoardo pointed to the fixtures in the main bathroom. They were outdated and cracked. "New?"

Reluctantly, Paolo nodded yes. They needed to be replaced.

Edoardo took him to the guest bathroom and pointed to the cracked tile. "New?"

Paolo shook his head no.

Edoardo raised a brow. "Not expensive. Better."

Paolo hesitated and then agreed to re-tiling the second bath.

They returned to the living room, and Edoardo paused. "*Grande problema,*" he began, shaking his head as he pointed to some foundation issues they had uncovered. "*Guarda* – look," he said, pointing to cracks in the floor. "New floor. *Bella. Elegante.* Porcelain but look like marble."

Paolo didn't want beautiful or elegant. He wanted basic and inexpensive.

"*Quanto?*" Paolo asked.

"*Diecimila.*"

"Ten thousand euro!" Paolo exclaimed.

Edoardo wiped beads of sweat off his brow. "Sell house. *Ventimila*. Make money."

Paolo didn't want to make money, but he had to admit the floors looked bad. If he had to repair them anyway, he might as well do them well and gain in the process. "Okay," he began. "But *basta* – enough, finish, no more."

Edoardo nodded, concealing a grin as he glanced down at the floor.

Paolo peered at Edoardo and asked, "Anything else?"

"No. *Basta cosi.*"

"Yes. *Basta cosi* – good enough with these changes. I'm going to go clean the cellar."

"Light?"

"Possible?"

"Yes. Generator. *Ci penso io.*"

Edoardo excused himself and fetched some wire to connect the cellar to the generator to provide Paolo with lighting. Edoardo and Paolo retraced steps to the cellar, and Edoardo found the separate electrical system. He connected the extension cord and turned on the generator. Inside the cellar, Paolo watched as the old lights flickered on and off. Finally, they remained lit. The space had a warm, ethereal feel.

Farther back in the barn-like structure, the stainless-steel vats for making wine gleamed in the light. Paolo recalled Angelo saying they were in good shape, but he wasn't sure what was involved. He had been with his grandfather several times as he crushed grapes and let them ferment, but it seemed like it was an art, one he had no aptitude or patience for.

In the front of the cellar, although the interior walls were made of stone, they were covered with wooden shelves and paneling to accommodate tools and storage. Deeper in the cavernous space, stone was abundant and arched beautifully overhead. In the soft yellow lights, the space looked like an expensive wine cellar. There were stacks of oak barrels, and farther back, racks of wine bottles. Paolo walked along the rows covered in dust. He picked up a bottle, ran his hand over the grime, and noticed the handwritten label – Minetti 2012 – *Trebbiano e Malvasia*. "Hmm," he murmured to himself. "I wonder if this is any good."

Paolo searched for an opener and found an old rusty one. He pressed it into the cork, twisted it, and opened the bottle, hearing the characteristic pop. He lowered his nose to the bottle. It didn't smell bad, although it was clearly older than most drinkable white wine. He walked outside and into the back of the house, searching the cabinets for a glass. He found one and poured the straw-colored liquid into it. Swirling it around a bit, he lifted the glass to his lips and took a sip. It had a mineral taste at first, then evolved to a smooth pear-like flavor. It was crisp, almost citrusy. "Not bad," he remarked. "It's old but has held up nicely."

He returned to the cellar and realized it might be a nice selling point for the villa. But it needed cleaning. He found some brushes, rags, and brooms and began to work from the back forward, dusting the bottles and sweeping the floor.

There were bottles in his grandfather's collection dating back to 2007. Paolo assumed most of the older whites had gone bad, but the younger ones might still be okay. There were several rows of Tuscan reds that he imagined were aging nicely.

The stone walls were beautiful and needed very little attention. They had been set with hardly any mortar, perfectly cut and arranged artistically. There were a few areas with a thin covering of plaster, and Paolo wondered if, at one time, the walls had been covered and painted.

The floor was somewhat moist and seemed more like hardened soil than stone. He brushed the floor with a broom, but each pass only left the same substrate intact. The surface was clearly something that had formed over the decades as dirt and debris were packed down. Paolo recalled that some ancient structures were carved out of tufa, a volcanic material, and wondered if it might be the case that the cellar had been initially carved out of something like that. He returned to the front of the cellar and retrieved a shovel so that he might scrape off the upper layer. In the deepest part of the cellar, he thrust the shovel into the material. It was light and dirt-like, not hard or volcanic. But he hit something rigid, stone-like, underneath. He scraped away more of the soil and discovered what looked like a subsurface of some sort.

Paolo walked forward a bit, thrust the shovel into the soil, and hit the same material. He cleared the dirt between the two places and found that an undersurface stretched between them.

"Hmm," he began. "Looks like there's a floor below."

Paolo went to the front of the cellar and retrieved a wheelbarrow. He began shoveling the debris into it. Gradually, the underflooring came to light, and he realized it was a mosaic.

"Well, I'll be! I never knew this was under here. I wonder if *nonno* knew about it."

Paolo continued to uncover the floor, dumping the dirt near the front of the cellar. At one point, as he walked outside, a car came up the drive. It was Angelo.

Angelo jumped out of the front seat and walked toward Paolo, extending his hand. "*Buongiorno*," he said. "How's the renovation going?"

"Fine," Paolo said without much excitement. "As I predicted, it's going to take longer and cost more."

Angelo shook his head, concerned that his new client was already disappointed with his advice.

"So, what are you up to? Can I invite you to lunch, discuss some real estate matters?"

"I'm dirty."

"Hmm, yes. It would seem you've gotten into the spirit of things!"

Paolo didn't chuckle. He stared at Angelo, who began to perspire in the heat.

"Let me show you something," Paolo said, leading him toward the cellar. "I got the tractor to work the other day and cleared the soil between the vines. I was in the process of cleaning the cellar when I discovered there is a floor underneath the debris."

Angelo gave him a curious look. "Let's see."

Paolo led him back into the cellar. "See. Below approximately 40 centimeters of soil, there's a mosaic. I wonder if my grandfather put it down or perhaps never knew it existed."

Angelo bent down and ran his hand over the surface of the mosaic floor. He took out his phone, turned on the spotlight, and peered at it more closely.

"Hmm," he murmured. "Very unusual."

"How so?"

"It's a bit uneven. If your grandfather had put it down, it would have a modern appearance. Contemporary mosaics are manufactured and have no irregularities. These look almost as if they are hand-cut, as if they might be ancient."

Paolo raised his brows in excitement. "That would be cool. An ancient Roman floor."

"Not cool," Angelo said. "If it's historic, you have to report it to the authorities. If that happens, all renovations have to stop, and you have to wait until the site can be excavated."

Paolo's face turned ashen. "You're kidding."

Angelo nodded his head no. He brushed more soil off the mosaic and peered at it. "Yep, this doesn't seem modern."

Angelo took the shovel and cleared more soil from the mosaic. While much of it was white, there were decorative lines and patterns that covered the periphery. It was undoubtedly an old Roman mosaic.

"Why would there be a mosaic here?" Paolo inquired with a knot in his stomach.

"This area was a rich agricultural region for ancient Rome. Just like today, there were villas for the wealthy Romans who retreated for fresh air, particularly in the summer. The ancient town of Tusculum was nearby, and there were quite a few sumptuous villas in the area. Frascati grew up when the ancient town and later medieval village were abandoned."

"So, my grandfather's villa might be sitting on the ruins of an ancient one?"

"Quite possibly. That would be remarkable."

Paolo shook his head. He knew this would mean an interminable delay in unloading the property. "What does this mean in terms of the sale of the property?"

"Nothing can take place until archaeologists investigate and determine what is here and whether anything needs to be excavated."

"What do we do in the meantime?"

"Nothing."

"Can we just cover it up?"

"You could, but if future buyers discover it and suspect you hid it, the sale would be null and void and you would be charged with crimes."

"Shit! How do I deal with the taxes and the renovations that are now in process?"

"We'll have to wait and see."

"How long will that take?"

"It could be quite some time, depending on the schedule of the superintendent of archaeology."

"A month or two?"

"Longer," Angelo said, knowing the news would set his client off. He looked off evasively.

Paolo exclaimed. "*Cazzo!* Fuck!"

Angelo's eyes widened. It was the first Italian word he had heard Paolo use.

"We need to report this. I also know someone who is an archaeologist. I can ask him for a favor and see if he will come sooner than later and assess things."

Paolo's shoulders relaxed. "That would be very nice of you."

"I'll do what I can. I can't promise anything."

"So, what do we tell Edoardo and his crew?"

"I'll share the bad news. I'll pay them for the couple of days' work they've done and send you an invoice. Do you want to grab lunch afterwards?"

"No, I'm not hungry now. I will go back to the hotel and do some work. I didn't need this on top of everything else."

"Keep a positive attitude. Maybe it's not a big deal and you can proceed. I'll go talk to the crew and give you a call later about a date with the archaeologist."

"Thanks," Paolo said.

Angelo spoke with the crew, who gathered their tools and sped off. Angelo got into his car and returned to his office. Paolo closed the cellar doors, locked them, and proceeded back to Frascati to his hotel room, where he showered and began to do some work on his computer.

Chapter Five – The Archaeologist

Two days later, Paolo sat in his car at the villa waiting for Angelo and the archaeologist. He had resigned himself to a delay and arranged a transfer from his parents' account to the local municipality to pay the back taxes. He hoped his parents wouldn't exhaust funds before he was able to complete the renovations and sell the property.

Paolo remained stressed. He wanted to unload the burden of the property and return to his life and work in Boston, and he feared that a long excavation of the site would throw all his plans into disarray. He noticed Angelo turn onto the driveway and approach the house. Paolo got out of his car and waited for them.

Angelo parked under the shade of one of the umbrella pines and stepped out of the driver's seat. The passenger got out too. They both walked toward Paolo.

Although thirty years had passed, the man accompanying Angelo was immediately recognizable. Paolo couldn't believe his eyes and wondered what trick the gods were playing. Although older, the man had aged well. The intriguing adolescent body had given way to an adult one — mature and classy. His frame was still tall and slender, his shoulders broad, and his head remained covered in dark, playful hair.

Paolo studied his face, searching for the expressive eyes and the enchanting dimples that had infatuated him before. Instead, the man's orbs were filled with disbelief.

"Paul, this is the archaeologist I mentioned who agreed to take a look at the mosaic. Mauro, this is Paul Minetti. Paul, this is Mauro Prato."

"Yes, we've met," Mauro said in a slow, measured voice as he extended his hand, unable to take his eyes off of Paolo. Paolo managed a feeble handshake.

Angelo gave them both a quizzical look.

"*Molti anni fa*," Mauro added, still peering at Paolo. "Thirty or so years ago, right?"

Paolo gave a nod. "My grandfather invited Mauro in the summers to enjoy the pool."

"Ah!" Angelo said. "What a coincidence."

"*Sì*, quite a surprising coincidence," Mauro added, clearly caught off guard. It was only when he and Angelo had turned off the main road that he realized he was heading to Carlo's estate.

Angelo continued to scrutinize the two of them, who stood motionless before each other.

"So, you're an archaeologist?" Paolo asked, searching for a thread of conversation.

"Hmm. Yes." Mauro answered nervously. "And you?"

Paolo didn't respond. He tilted his head a bit, as if it sufficed for an answer.

"So, when was the last time?" Mauro asked.

"I think it was 1995 or so, if I recall," Paolo replied as if guessing, although the exact year was indelibly etched in his mind.

Mauro nodded.

"So," Paolo interjected, unable to think of anything else to say. "We seem to have a potential problem with a mosaic I uncovered in the cellar."

Mauro, relieved at the segue, said, "Yes. Let's take a look."

All three walked toward the cellar. Mauro scrutinized Paolo from behind. Everything felt surreal — the terrain under his feet, the looming wooden doors of the cellar, and the tussled hair of the enigmatic grandson Carlo used to talk about all the time.

Paolo paused at the entrance of the cellar and glanced back at Mauro and Angelo. Mauro felt his legs grow weak as their eyes connected. As a teen, he had always longed for such a moment, one in which Paolo saw him, recognized him, might nod in affirmation of an affinity of sorts, although he wasn't sure what that was. While Paolo's eyes lacked generosity, they were at least curious. The inimical and cold indifference of the past had given way to eyes filled with interest and wonder — what became of you, where did you go, why are you here now? Mauro trembled at the possible answers that swirled in his head, realizing that seeing Paolo stirred feelings he thought he had buried long ago.

Paolo opened the doors wide. He had purchased several battery-operated lanterns and took Angelo and Mauro toward the back area. Although the underground stone walls cooled the air, Paolo felt nervous perspiration trickle down his chest and back, moistening the top of his briefs. He glanced back at Angelo and Mauro as they followed, shaking his head in disbelief.

Mauro glanced around the familiar structure. He had driven the tractor for Carlo, had helped process grapes, had tested vintages, and fully expected Carlo to leap out of a corner and give him a big hug.

Paolo stopped in the back section of the cellar and said, "Here's where I began to remove a heavy layer of dirt from the floor. I discovered the mosaic underneath. When Angelo saw it, he thought the tiles were old. Maybe they aren't. Maybe someone wanted to create the impression of an ancient floor," he proffered, hoping against all hope that they didn't have historical value.

Mauro stepped forward and leaned down, running his hand over the surface. Paolo held the lantern up over his head to provide illumination. He scrutinized the back of Mauro's head and the contours of his shoulders pressed against the fabric of his shirt. He was handsome. Paolo felt his heart flutter.

Mauro pulled a trowel out of his shoulder bag and scraped the area. His eyes focused on the decorative patterns at the edge — colorful tiles depicting vines, grapes, and the harvest. "Hmm," he murmured. "I would be curious to know what lies beyond the decorative border. If it's just an expanse of white tile, it might be old but not that significant. However, since this is in an area where there were many sumptuous Roman villas, it might include images with more artistic value. We will only know after it is excavated."

Paolo felt his heart skip a beat. He hesitatingly began, "So, it has to be excavated?"

Mauro stood and stared at Paolo. "I'm afraid so."

"How long does that take?"

"It depends on the size of the floor and when we are able to get a team here to do the work. It could be years."

"Years?" Paolo said with alarm.

Mauro nodded, and Angelo raised his brows as he gave Paolo a concerned look.

Mauro didn't feel sympathy for Paolo. During the summer of 1995, Paolo had been unfriendly, self-absorbed, and seemingly unappreciative of his heritage, the affection of his grandparents, and the social opportunities around him.

"Mauro, does the renovation of the house have to stop?" Angelo asked, hoping to convey some sense of his concern for Paolo's predicament.

"Unfortunately, yes. Until we determine the extent of the site, we can't risk damage to other historic elements that might be underground."

"Shit," Paolo said, shaking his head.

"Mauro, are there any teams that might be able to come out and assess things sooner than later?" Angelo asked.

Mauro shook his head. "I'm not aware of any. Most of them have projects lined up months and years in advance."

"What if I just cover the floor back up, and the work on the house remains cosmetic, surface?"

Mauro glanced at Angelo, and they both glanced at Paolo. "I'm afraid once something like this has been brought to light, it can't be covered over. It must be reported. Violations of the site carry large penalties."

"Fuck this country!" Paolo said, kicking one of the wine racks with force. As the bottles shook, Angelo and Mauro raised their brows in alarm.

There was a protracted, uncomfortable silence and then Angelo asked Mauro, "Do you need to see anything else?"

Mauro shook his head silently. He and Angelo headed toward the cellar door, and Paolo followed, muttering to himself.

Outside, Angelo and Mauro waited as Paolo fussed with the locks and doors. "That went well," Angelo whispered to Mauro, chuckling quietly.

"It doesn't surprise me," Mauro remarked, glancing over his shoulder to make sure Paolo wasn't nearby. "He's always been moody and excitable."

"I didn't realize," Angelo noted. "Sorry you had to revisit that."

"It's okay. We get that a lot when we visit new sites. No one is happy with the delay and additional costs incurred while excavations go on."

"Paolo, or I should say Paul, was hoping to unload this quickly."

"That's not going to happen."

"Here he comes," Angelo whispered.

Paolo walked out into the light. His face was red with anger.

Mauro walked up to him and said, "We'll see what we can do to speed things up for you. But I can't make any promises."

Paolo just nodded.

"It was a surprise to see you again," Mauro added, extending his hand.

Paolo shook his hand. "Yes. Quite a surprise. Here's my card in case you have any news to share."

Mauro took the card and scrutinized it. He nodded to Paolo and glanced at Angelo, ready to leave.

"You ready to head back to the station?" Angelo asked Mauro.

"Yes. Thanks. *Ciao*," he said to Paolo as they walked toward Angelo's car.

As they drove down the driveway to the main road, Angelo said, "I didn't realize you and Paolo knew each other."

"It's an interesting story."

"I have time. There's a nice café near the station, if you want to share."

"Sure. I could use a drink!"

Angelo laughed.

In town, Angelo parked the car, and they walked to a small tree-covered plaza. There were small iron tables set in the shade, and a white-aproned server ran back and forth, serving sandwiches and drinks. Mauro and Angelo found a free table and nodded to the server, who came and took their order.

Angelo reached into his jacket, pulled out a packet of cigarettes, lit one, and offered one to Mauro. "*Vuoi?*"

"No thanks. I don't smoke," Mauro replied.

"So, you and Paolo. Sounds like quite a history. Tell me all about it," Angelo began as he leaned forward, taking a long drag of his cigarette.

"Well, the last time I saw Paolo was in 1995, I think. We were both seventeen. His grandfather invited me to the villa to meet Paolo and swim. I think Carlo took pity on me. My stepfather was abusive, and Carlo wanted to get me away from him. I welcomed the reprieve."

"Paolo doesn't seem to like the villa or Italy. What happened?"

"From the moment I met him, it was clear he was unhappy. He sulked around the grounds and the pool, hidden behind his dark glasses and closed off in the world of his CD player and American music."

"What is that all about? I can't believe he wants to unload the villa. He seems to despise it and everything Italian. He goes by Paul and pretends he doesn't speak Italian, but I can tell from the expressions on his face that he fully comprehends what is being said."

"He did the same thing when we were younger. His grandparents spoke to him in Italian, and he responded to them in English. I know he understood them. The others Carlo invited — cousins and locals — all spoke to Paolo in Italian. He would stare at them as if he comprehended nothing. They walked away from him disappointed, not realizing it was all an act."

"So why do you think he dislikes it so much here?" Angelo inquired.

"I don't know. I tried to pry it out of his grandfather, but he made excuses for him — that he was shy, that he felt uncomfortable with the language, or was homesick. There must have been something else going on."

"Like?"

"I don't know. Given Carlo's warmth and caring, I can't imagine he had been abusive to Paolo. Paolo's parents, whom I met a couple of times, seemed equally nice."

"Did he make any friends while he was here?"

"I never remember seeing him laugh or have a conversation with people Carlo invited — all of them Paolo's age."

"Did you and Paolo talk?"

"Rarely. However," Mauro began, stopping in mid-sentence.

Mauro didn't continue. He stared off into the distance as if in thought. Angelo asked, "However what?"

"I don't know. Paolo and I didn't visit. We exchanged necessary information having to do with visitors, food, towels, and other practical matters. At first, I was hurt and disappointed. After getting to know Carlo and Luisa, I became angry that Paolo was so ungrateful to them. But over the summer, I just let it go. I wish we could have become friends, but it wasn't going to happen. I always thought there was some hidden agenda, something under the surface."

Angelo gave Mauro a curious look.

Mauro continued, looking off into the distance as if in thought. "In retrospect, I wonder if we were each secretly jealous of the other."

"How so?"

"My home and family were not happy. I longed to have what Paolo had, to be who Paolo was — the grandson of this larger-than-life kind of man with a villa, a vineyard, and a pool in the countryside."

"And Paolo?"

"I don't know. I get the feeling that his antipathy toward all things Italian had to do with something else. Deep down, I think he was intrigued by me. I caught him glancing in my direction from time to time, as if he were studying me and trying to uncover something. His gaze often lingered, particularly around the pool. But it was unaccompanied by any interaction. I could never figure him out."

As Mauro described and recreated things in his head, the thought came to him that perhaps Paolo, as indifferent as he came across, actually harbored desires for him. He grinned at the idea, realizing that perhaps he was onto Paolo's secret.

"So, how did things end?"

"As the summer progressed, we engaged less and less. Paolo was always at the far end of the pool, reclining on the chaise, and listening to his blasted American music. He would nod in my direction from time to time, but we exchanged few words."

"That must have been awkward."

"Very. I decided not to return, but Carlo insisted, fabricating all sorts of reasons why he needed me to visit and help him with work."

"And Paolo never showed embarrassment that it was you, not he, who helped his grandfather."

"None. It was the oddest thing."

"Then what?"

"Things ended unceremoniously. Late in August, I heard from Carlo that Paolo was returning to Boston. I left, and when I returned several days later, he was gone. No words of goodbye or farewell or anything of the sort. It was as if I didn't exist, as if he had never existed."

"Did you keep up with his grandfather?"

"I made visits several times after that summer. Carlo and Luisa were always so warm and welcoming, and it was a pleasant contrast to my own home. When I went off to the university, we lost touch. I ended up marrying and, well, apart from one short visit, hadn't been back until today."

"Did Paolo ever come back?"

"Not during the immediate years. I have no idea if he came back later."

"So, the mosaics. What do you think?"

"They are Roman and probably of historic value, considering the kind of Roman villas that existed in this area. The question is how extensive the flooring is and whether there are other architectural elements under the house or the land."

"And we are talking a while before work could begin?"

Mauro nodded. There was an almost imperceptible grin on his face. Angelo noticed and grinned back.

Angelo drummed his fingers on the table, deep in thought. He, too, didn't mind seeing Paolo squirm a bit. But he also wanted to make a sale and hoped something more expeditious might be possible.

"Are there any hands to grease? I'd like to move this along."

"I'm afraid not. But I'll see if there's anything I can do."

"I'd be grateful."

Mauro smiled. Then he added thoughtfully, "It's amazing how destiny brings people and places together."

"*Si. Veramente!* Truly."

"Well, it's been a pleasure and a surprise. I'm sure we will see each other again soon."

"I hope so. *Ciao.*"

The two shook hands, and Mauro headed to the station, where he caught a train back to Rome.

6

Chapter Six – Photos

Paolo watched as Mauro and Angelo sped off down the driveway. He went inside the house and retrieved the box of photos he had found a few days earlier. He got into his own car and headed to town.

Once inside his hotel room, he sat on the sofa and opened the box. He trembled as he began to remove layers of pictures — most of them of his grandparents with their friends, of Carlo testing a new vintage, or of Luisa making sauce in the kitchen. He dug deeper and found several slightly faded color photographs of young people around the pool. Paolo's heart began to pound in his chest as he studied them.

He held up one and peered closely, trying to identify everyone. It was a large group of darkly tanned teenagers — all scantily clad in swimsuits. "There's Joanna," he murmured to himself, recognizing his grandmother's great-niece. "And Tomaso and Gabriella. Hmm," he muttered, realizing they had been a couple that summer. He searched the people in the back row for Mauro. He wasn't there.

Rummaging deeper in the pile of photographs, Paolo pulled out another. His grandmother must have taken the picture. Carlo was in the middle of a group of teenage girls sipping lemonade and eating cookies. The image had captured Carlo's mischievous eyes and the delight he obviously felt at having so many young people around. He stared at them affectionately, and they were laughing in return. In the back of the picture, Paolo noticed himself, phantom-like and awkward. He remembered feeling so inadequate and out-of-place.

After placing the picture on the side table, he dug for more. There were several shots of Carlo on the tractor, and one of Paolo's parents — Enzo and Rita — helping Luisa in the kitchen. In another, the five of them posed for a snapshot in front of the local parish. He must have been eight or nine.

There was another picture of Luisa tending the garden, and Carlo shaking hands with a neighbor. He picked one out of the stack, a cute one of him, Paolo, riding a bicycle down the driveway. There seemed to be no order to the prints — older ones mixed with newer. His grandmother had a formal album in Boston; these seemed like a mishmash of shots taken casually and thrown into a box.

At the bottom of the collection there was a crinkled print, one that was rather discolored. It looked as if it had been handled frequently. Not believing his eyes, Paolo held it up to the light and examined it carefully. "What the fuck!" he exclaimed.

There he was — arm and arm with Mauro. A pose he had forgotten, a moment that should have been memorable but had faded like so many other troubling encounters. They were at the edge of the pool. It must have been late in the summer as their bodies were dark from the sun. Paolo chuckled as he observed how stiff and unhappy he looked in the setting. Mauro was relaxed, standing *contrapposto*, smiling warmly. His right arm was slung over Paolo's shoulder. Mauro's swimsuit was loose, the drawstring untied and part of the fabric hanging off his hip, showing his tan line. It was terribly sexy.

Turning the image over, Paolo read out loud, "1995 – By the pool."

Paolo turned it back over and scrutinized the two of them. "Man, we looked good," he murmured to himself, lamenting how long it had been since he had such a thin waist, lean abdomen, or muscular torso. He kept glancing at Mauro's swimsuit — so provocative and seductive. He tried to recall the moment. He, Paolo, looked annoyed. Perhaps it had been a mask he invented to conceal his desire, his obsession, his fascination with Mauro's body. He remembered fearing Carlo would uncover his secret and shame him, or worse still, send some scantily clad teenage girl in his direction, pointing out all her attributes. It was the fear of that that nurtured a well-choreographed strategy of indifference and introversion. He vowed that no one should ever know his secret.

Paolo dropped the photo back into the box of pictures, placing it on a side table in the room.

A few days later, Paolo received a call from Mauro.

"Hello," Paolo responded when he picked up the call.

"Paolo, this is Mauro. *Come stai?*"

Paolo hesitated, annoyed that Mauro again presumed upon his Italian. But he needed Mauro to be helpful, so he responded to Mauro's question. "Good. What can I do for you?"

"I'm calling to see if we could meet and discuss some information and options about the villa and the mosaic floor."

"I hope you have good news," Paolo said emphatically.

Mauro held the phone away from his ear and gave it a stern look. He whispered to himself, "*Stronzo* –asshole!" Then he continued, "There are some opportunities. I would like to go over them with you."

"What do you have in mind?"

"We could meet for dinner someplace — either in Frascati or Rome."

"Why don't I come into the city? It's pretty boring out here," Paolo said.

"Are you free tomorrow? We could meet around seven. I know a nice restaurant in the historic center. I will text you directions."

"Sounds good. See you tomorrow."

"*A presto.*"

Paolo almost said, '*si*,' but caught himself and said, "See you tomorrow."

Paolo fell back in the comfortable chair of his hotel room, reached for the glass of wine on the coffee table, and took a long sip. He opened his laptop and clicked on the links he had found of Mauro, his family, and his work. He enlarged the photo in his profile and peered at his thoughtful and restless eyes. The image must have been taken at a dig. Bright sun illuminated pillars in the background. He wore cargo shorts, a linen shirt, and a broad-brimmed hat.

His work as an archaeologist made sense. He remembered him as an inquiring and probing person, someone trying to figure things out, uncover things hidden and concealed.

As he scrutinized the website, he regretted having agreed to dinner. It would have been more straightforward and less complicated to have Mauro come to the villa and go over options. Dinner was bound to be filled with reminiscences and rehashing of years past, an emotional minefield Paolo wanted to avoid.

The next afternoon, Paolo prepared for his visit to Rome. He found his heart racing as he tried on various polo shirts, searching for just the right color and look. He turned to the side, pulling in his stomach and extending his chest. "Hmm," he mumbled to himself. He realized that while he was caring for his grandparents and parents, he had let himself go. He stared closely into the mirror and ran his hand through his dark hair. He raised his brow and turned his head slightly. His parents and grandparents always took hold of his cheeks and said, "*Faccia bella!*" He did have a handsome face, but he worried about the rest of the package — the sagging jeans, the loose sleeves, and the lack of any definition in his chest. He chuckled at himself, at his attempt to make a good impression on Mauro. It wasn't as if he hoped something might come of their meeting. He just didn't want Mauro to think he had been a loser over the years.

Later, he boarded the train in Frascati for the main station in Rome and gazed out the window as the train traversed the verdant countryside. Everything felt unreal, dreamlike — being in Italy, on a train, heading to Rome, to see a teenage acquaintance. Most would have pegged him as a local, but he felt out-of-place heading to the city. He never recalled going to Rome much during his childhood years. The vineyard took a lot of work, and his grandparents preferred the tranquil countryside to the bustling city.

Once at Termini, a chaotic station filled with tourists, locals, and petty thieves taking advantage of so many distractions, he grabbed his shoulder bag and picked up a taxi outside. The driver raced through the streets and left him a few blocks away from the pedestrian area of the historical center. The Largo Argentina was a busy crossroads surrounding an excavation site filled with ancient Roman temples — small ones, very old ones. He had read that within the same archaeological site, just behind some of the religious structures, were the remains of the Curia of Pompey, where Julius Caesar had been assassinated. He peered down at the ruins, raised a brow, and then glanced at his phone, where he had saved a map to the restaurant.

The pedestrian street leading into the historical center was wide and lined with venerable historic palaces. He faced a torrent of people moving toward him, heading home from work, eager to join friends at a café, or chasing school kids kicking soccer balls through the crowd. Down the street, the late afternoon sun cast a beautiful glow on the orange and ochre walls. Paolo paused in front of the façade of a plain-looking church, where a local guide gesticulated excitedly in front of a group of tourists. The guide stated passionately, "This complex was where the trial of Galileo took place in 1633. The Inquisition questioned him for his belief that the Earth rotated on its axis, something the church leaders feared contradicted scripture and challenged their authority. It was only in 1992 that Pope John Paul II finally apologized for the Church's treatment of him, suggesting that when there is a contradiction between clear and certain reason and scripture, we have to follow the evidence of reason and find new ways of interpreting scripture."

The tourists glanced at one another and nodded, apparently in agreement with the more modern sentiments. The guide continued, "Inside the church, there are a couple of things to note. It is here that the body of St. Catherine of Siena is found under the altar. She was active in helping resolve a crisis in the Middle Ages when there were several men claiming to be Pope at the same time. She was also a prolific writer of theology and considered one of the more important mystics of the Church. Next to the altar, when you are inside, you will see a large statue of the resurrected Christ. It is one of Michelangelo's works and was originally a nude, underscoring the restoration of human innocence after Jesus' death and resurrection. It represents one of the high points of Christian humanism — the celebration of humanity in all of its nobility and grandeur. Let's go inside and take a look."

While the guide's speech intrigued Paolo who knew very little of Roman history, and while he was surprised at so many pivotal events and people represented in such a small patch of Rome, he still felt a deep antipathy for it all — another old church here, a curious story there, and a few modestly interesting pieces of art. He continued to wonder what all the fuss was about.

As the group headed toward the entrance of the church, Paolo continued toward the Piazza Rotonda. The curved outer walls of the Pantheon loomed overhead as he walked down the street. He walked past the towering columns holding up the porch of the temple dedicated to all the gods and gazed up at the dome, partially concealed by the porch.

The square was full of people, many lined up to go inside the structure and others chatting with neighbors or sitting in cafes, sipping cocktails, wine, and coffee. Paolo pivoted in place, taking in the myriad colors of the surrounding medieval buildings, the sound of an accordion echoing off the walls, and the smell of roasted coffee and ancient stone foundations wafting in the air. He wanted to dislike it all, but there was a certain enchantment to it that he found hard to dismiss.

Paolo chuckled at the tourists fanning themselves as they waited for their turn to see the inside of the Pantheon. He wondered why people would pay big bucks to fly to Italy only to be pressed and squeezed by countless other tourists to get a glimpse of an old building? He did a quick search on his phone to see why there was so much interest in the monument. He discovered that the Pantheon was approximately nineteen hundred years old and that until modern times, it had been the largest dome in the world. He read that architects still marvel at its design — one where the height and width are equal, creating an expansive effect on people when they walk inside.

Paolo glanced up at the building and realized that he really should go inside, that he should be curious — but he felt no urge, interest, or desire. Wandering through a maze of irregular streets and alleys, Paolo found the restaurant Mauro had selected. It was a small trattoria with a large awning stretched over a dozen tables. Mauro waved from a side table, rose, and approached Paolo, extending his hand warmly.

"*Ciao, Paolo.*"

"Hello, Mauro," Paolo replied, making sure Mauro knew the meeting would be conducted in English.

Mauro furrowed his brow and pointed toward the table. "Come, have a seat. Would you like some wine?"

"I've become more of a beer drinker. Do they serve beer?"

"Of course." Mauro caught the attention of the server and ordered Paolo a beer. It didn't surprise him that Paolo preferred beer. It fit the pattern of distancing himself from his roots.

When it came, they raised their glasses and said, "Cheers."

"I have to say, this is very surreal," Mauro began. "Angelo mentioned someone needed a site visit. I had no idea it would be Carlo's place and that you would be there."

"I was as surprised as you."

They both stared at their drinks nervously, unsure of which direction to take the conversation.

Paolo added, "I looked you up. Sounds like you have been quite successful as an archaeologist. And I see you are married."

"Ah, yes. I met Anna during an excavation in Turkey. We married soon thereafter. We have a daughter, Emilia, who is 22 and a teacher in Modena."

"Congratulations."

Mauro felt blood rush to his face. He didn't trust Paolo's efforts to be friendly or gracious. "And you?" Mauro inquired.

"I'm a fund manager in Boston. As you might have surmised, Carlo and Luisa have passed. My parents are alive but in poor health. I came to sell the property."

"Any family?"

"No. Just me."

Mauro raised his brow and took a deep breath.

"Why do you want to sell the villa? It's such a beautiful property."

"It was never my thing."

Paolo's response wasn't surprising. He had hoped that perhaps over the years Paolo might have developed some interest in his past. He hadn't.

"Shall we order some appetizers?" Mauro asked, glancing at the menu.

"I'm not that hungry. What news do you have to share?"

Mauro didn't raise his head. He hoped that by not looking at Paolo, his rude impertinence might miraculously vanish or shift into something more civil and social. He asked, "How about a caprese salad and some prosciutto and melon?"

Paolo nodded, resigned to the typical circumambulation of things in Italy. No one got right down to business. Transactions were always preceded by small talk, conversation about inane things — like the weather, municipal problems, new restaurants, wine, vacations, and family gossip.

Mauro ordered the appetizers and took an evasive sip of wine. He sensed Paolo was eager to hear what he had to share, so he began, "Well, I spoke to some colleagues. Apparently, there's a group of American graduate students looking for a project. The one they had come to work on has unexpected complications, so they are free. It is very unusual for an opportunity like this to appear so late in the season, but it might work out for you."

Paolo's shoulders relaxed, and he leaned toward Mauro to hear more.

"Don't get too excited. These things are complicated. First, they will do some ultrasound tests of the area to determine the extent of the floor and whether there are any other structures under the surface of the property. They will map out the terrain and then make a proposal for work."

"That's good news, right?"

"It depends."

"Do you think it's extensive — that things that will need to be excavated?"

"No one knows. There were a lot of sumptuous villas in the area back in Roman times. Between earthquakes, pillage, and neglect, many disappeared. Some were incorporated into medieval and Renaissance structures. Others were buried. Many were pilfered, their treasures used in newer buildings. I vaguely recall some interesting pillars in your grandfather's house. It's possible there's a large structure underneath or, alternatively, nothing much — that most of the valuable things were taken away ages ago."

"So, when could this crew begin?"

"I get the impression they are eager to start. Maybe in a couple of weeks. We have to process the paperwork."

Paolo smiled. It was the first time he expressed any modicum of delight.

"What do I need to do?"

"Nothing at the moment. If you need to go back to Boston, I can coordinate work at the villa."

The server brought the appetizers to the table. The caprese salad looked just like the ones Luisa used to make in Frascati, and a tear formed in Paolo's eye. He concealed it carefully with a sip of his drink and a casual swipe of his napkin over his face.

"This looks delicious," Mauro remarked. "Would you like another beer?"

Paolo studied his glass. A few centimeters of amber liquid remained at the bottom. "I'll switch to wine, if you don't mind."

"Not at all. I have a bottle of Trebbiano, here. Would you like some?"

Paolo nodded, too emotional to say yes. It was the same varietal his grandfather used to make.

"So, a fund manager. I would never have guessed," Mauro said, hoping to shift the topic to something more interpersonal.

"Why?"

"I don't know," Mauro began. In fact, Mauro thought, fund manager perfectly suited the quiet, cerebral, insolent Paolo. But it was still surprising. "I would have thought you would have pursued music or literature, or something in the humanities. You were always buried in books and music."

"Hmm," Paolo muttered, surprised that Mauro had been paying attention to him years ago. "Life surprises us."

"Indeed."

"Why archaeology?"

"I had a college professor who inspired me. I realized I liked history, art, and puzzles. I also liked being outdoors, not cooped up in an office."

"You said you met your wife in Turkey. Where?"

"We were doing excavations in Sardis."

Paolo furrowed his forehead as he pierced a piece of mozzarella cheese and tomato and put it in his mouth. The explosion of flavors — the heirloom tomatoes, the soft cheese, and the fresh basil —

brought back memories of his childhood. He gave Mauro a curious look.

"Sardis is in a remote area, a bit east of Ephesus. It's a unique site with a large reconstructed Roman gymnasium, a very impressive ancient synagogue, a temple, and other interesting structures. Anna and I were working on the same team, and we grew fond of each other."

Paolo took an evasive sip of wine. The tales of Mauro's affections only reinforced Paolo's contempt for him. 'How sweet!' he wanted to remark with an exaggerated southern flair, but he held back and stated with little emotion, "She must be a special woman."

"She is. You will both have to meet sometime."

"I would like that," Paolo said disingenuously. He yearned for a quick resolution to the problem of the mosaic, so that he could sell the villa and be on his way back to Boston.

"Should we order something more substantial? Do you like veal chops? They are quite good here."

"I don't have a very sophisticated palate," Paolo replied. "I'll trust your recommendation."

Mauro caught the server's attention and ordered for them. When he turned back to the table, Paolo was deeply engrossed in texts on his phone. Mauro took the opportunity to steal a furtive look, to scrutinize the man before him. Paolo had a thick, sexy nose and an exceedingly handsome face — an angular jaw, deeply set brown eyes, and a broad forehead. Mauro fought competing emotions inside — disdain and obsession — and he wasn't sure which would eventually win.

When Paolo looked up, Mauro asked, "So, you never married?"

"No, I've been too busy with work and care of my grandparents and parents."

"Any close calls?"

Paolo wasn't sure how to answer. Mauro was married to Anna, and he wasn't ready to deal with the awkwardness of coming out to him. "Not really."

"Come on. A handsome guy like you?"

"Well, I guess there have been a few romances here and there."

"Tell me more."

"Another time."

Mauro was convinced there was more to the story, but let it drop.

"So, how did Carlo die? I'm sorry to hear of his and Luisa's passing."

"He had heart problems. He covered them up well, but they eventually caught up with him. It was six years ago."

"And Luisa?"

"Around the same time. They were so in love. I think his passing killed her."

"Why the delay in dealing with the house?"

"It took a while to sort things out — titles, trusts, and then my parents got ill."

"Sounds like a lot."

"You can't imagine."

Mauro looked off into the distance pensively.

The server brought their veal chops and potatoes, and both eagerly began to eat, grateful for a reprieve from questions and memories.

Paolo observed Mauro, watching the finesse at which he sliced his chop, the graceful way he took hold of his wineglass, and his overall poise. Classy, handsome, and pensive — they were killer qualities Paolo gravitated to. Mauro wore a peach-colored pullover that complemented his dark skin. The overhead patio lights cast a warm glow over the space, and Paolo felt himself being drawn inexorably toward Mauro, sensations he thought had been put to rest long ago.

Paolo wondered if Mauro had ever experimented; had ever drifted to the other side? Did he share inclinations, and how much wine might it take for them to surface? He reached over and poured Mauro another glass.

Mauro glanced up as Paolo poured the wine and caught his deep brown eyes peering in his direction. It only confirmed what he had suspected many years ago, that despite Paolo's apparent indifference, there was an underlying curiosity. They each held the gaze for a protracted moment, a connection that as teenagers would have been frightening and inadmissible, but which, now, held fascination and mounting questions.

"This is delicious," Paolo remarked, trying to minimize the import of their regard.

"It's one of my favorite restaurants," Mauro replied.

Paolo considered the remark and realized the selection of the venue for their dinner had not been accidental or casual.

"What does your wife do?" Paolo asked out of the blue.

Mauro glanced up, surprised at the question. "She is a teacher, but she's on leave."

Paolo returned a quizzical look.

"She's taking a break. The pressures of teaching are tough."

"She's not an archaeologist?"

"When we had our daughter, she didn't want to have to go on excavations, so she took up teaching."

"Ah," Paolo muttered, and pushed a few peas and potatoes around on his plate.

"I still remember the summer you came from the States," Mauro interjected, finally dipping his toes in an area of conversation he had been rehearsing all day.

"Hmm," Paolo said, nodding tentatively. "Not a happy time for me."

"Why?" Mauro asked. It was a question he had always wanted to ask.

"My friends all had jobs at local camps. I had to spend the summer with my grandparents in a foreign country."

"I would have thought that would have been exciting, exotic, fun!"

Paolo nodded no.

"Carlo and Luisa seemed to have so much fun inviting us over, feeding us, and letting us use the pool. We all thought you were so lucky to have such loving and interesting grandparents. I know I was jealous."

Paolo stared at Mauro and widened his eyes in disbelief.

"Yes. I was jealous," Mauro repeated emphatically.

Paolo wanted to say he was jealous of Mauro. Mauro was handsome and popular, and all the girls hovered over him. Instead, he said, "I can't see why."

"Come on, man. You were the American who could afford to fly to Italy and who had a collection of American CDs, books, and who spoke English. We all fantasized about your life."

"Of course I spoke English."

"You spoke English and Italian. All of us wanted to do the same."

"I don't speak Italian."

"You refuse to speak Italian."

Paolo glared at Mauro. Mauro was right, but Paolo didn't want to admit it. "Nevertheless, it was a horrible summer."

Mauro had hoped Paolo might have some fond memories; memories that had never been excavated — perhaps an affinity for something they shared. But he had hit a wall. Paolo was the same insufferable man he had met nearly thirty years ago. He wanted to confront Paolo about why he found Italy so awful, but he surmised the conversation wouldn't go well.

"I'm sorry to hear. Did you ever come back?"

"No."

"All these years, you never returned?"

Paolo nodded no.

"Why?"

"I guess it didn't hold much appeal. I was busy with college, then graduate school, then launching my career. It just never happened."

Mauro took a long sip of wine. He found Paolo's lack of interest in Italy disconcerting, as if it had something to do with him. He glanced up and hoped the same curious eyes might be looking in his direction. They weren't. Paolo was buried in his veal chop and glancing to the side of his plate at a text that had appeared on his phone. It was 1995 all over again. Less hostile, but still indifferent. Impossible to decipher. A handsome and enigmatic man, one he had hoped to make sense of long ago but who now seemed hopelessly entrenched in his ways.

Mauro quickly consumed the veal chop, realizing there wasn't much point in prolonging the evening.

Paolo looked up from time to time without comment, glancing off into the distance as if curiously studying the restaurant and the small square just beyond the awning. He wasn't really interested in the surroundings, he just feared that if his and Mauro's eyes connected, Mauro might detect a lingering fascination.

When they had finished their meals, neither expressed interest in ordering dessert or coffee. Mauro asked for the check and paid the bill. They stood awkwardly and walked into the piazza.

"Well, I should head back to Frascati."

"Hmm," Mauro replied. "I'll be in touch regarding next steps."

"Thanks," Paolo said, extending his hand.

Mauro shook Paolo's hand, savoring the warmth of his skin. Despite the unpleasantness of their evening together, the touch sent shivers up Mauro's arms — a touch he had always dreamed of and longed for but rarely had. As Paolo stepped into a nearby taxi and waved goodbye, Mauro held his hands together, preserving the lingering impressions on his skin.

Chapter Seven – The Vatican

The archaeological team Mauro had identified to help assess and excavate Paolo's mosaic was wrapping up some studies at the Vatican, and they wanted to meet Paolo in advance of their visit to the villa. Mauro arranged an appointment for them.

Paolo took a train to Rome and a taxi to the museum, where Mauro was waiting outside the entrance set within the massive stone walls of Vatican City.

"*Buongiorno*," Mauro said warmly as Paolo approached. He was glad to see him again. He had been struggling the last few days with an irrational fear that Paolo was perhaps only a phantom, a tempting but incorporeal apparition of a childhood acquaintance.

Paolo nodded, extended his hand, and said with little emotion, "Mauro." He glanced disdainfully at Mauro, dressed in a jacket, tie, and slacks. Everything about Mauro was conventional, official, bureaucratic.

"Let's go inside. The team is waiting," Mauro suggested.

They walked past throngs of tourists lined up for the day, all eager to see the treasures of the Vatican, particularly the Sistine Chapel. Paolo glanced around and continued to wonder what all the fuss was about.

"We're going to meet in an office inside. After our meeting, if you like, I can take you to other parts of the complex. If you haven't been in a while, there might be some favorite sections you would like to see again."

"I have to get back to Frascati after the meeting," Paolo replied emphatically.

"It's only nine in the morning. We'll be through by ten, and you have all day to kill."

"I have work back at the hotel."

"We're six hours ahead of Boston. Enough with the excuses. What's your favorite part of the museum?" Mauro asked, determined to penetrate Paolo's impervious shell. He had wrestled with conflicting emotions — contempt for the self-absorbed and spoiled American and a deeply buried curiosity or perhaps even infatuation with him. Years ago, they had exchanged few words. Paolo was now at his mercy, and he wanted to find out more, uncover the underlying narrative that might shed light on everything.

"Well," Paolo began tentatively. "I really don't have a favorite."

"The Raphael Rooms? Roman sculptures? Mosaics? Egyptian art? The Sistine Chapel? The painting gallery?"

Paolo made an almost imperceptible nod no.

Mauro opened his mouth wide in amazement. "You've never been to the museum before, have you?"

Paolo turned red with embarrassment.

"Well, then, we are going to have to change that. You know you are looking at one of the best guides!"

Paolo grinned, but he wasn't happy at the prospect of a protracted visit to the museum, much less having to listen to Mauro go on and on about Italian history and art.

They rounded a corner and went into a conference room, where a group of young graduate students sat in front of a projector. They stood as Mauro and Paolo entered the room.

The teacher approached Mauro and shook his hand. Frank, this is Paolo Minetti. Paolo, this is Frank Bonfiglio.

"Nice to meet you," Paolo said. "Call me Paul."

"And this is the team of graduate students who will be surveying and excavating your site." Frank said, pointing to the group assembled. They all nodded.

"Something to drink? Water? Coffee?"

"No, thanks."

"You must have been excited to find the mosaic."

"Thrilled," Paolo replied sarcastically, glaring at Mauro. "I'm hoping it's nothing of significance, so I can complete the renovation and sell the property."

Frank glanced at Mauro, who shook his head.

"And how did you find it?"

"Cleaning out the cellar floor."

"Amazing," Frank noted. "We were looking for a good project for these graduate students. This looks perfect — something manageable and perhaps groundbreaking."

Frank glanced at Paolo, hoping he might chuckle at the pun. Paolo looked restless, annoyed, and eager to get onto the agenda at hand. Mauro picked up on the pun, winked at Frank, and rolled his eyes at Paolo's indifference.

Cognizant of Paolo's irritability, Mauro interjected, "Perhaps we could review the project."

Frank had hoped for more pleasantries, but picked up on Mauro's not-so-subtle hint that things should move along. "Well. Yes. Let's take a look at the slide presentation. It lays out the steps we will follow to survey the property, make an assessment, and excavate things."

Everyone sat, Frank dimmed the lights, and the slide show commenced. It was a specialized presentation of archaeological tools and techniques. Paolo was interested, but his heart kept racing as he contemplated the implications of it all. When the show finished, Frank asked, "Any questions?"

Mauro interjected. "If I can speak for Paul, I know he is anxious to sell the property, as his parents are ill. Do you have any sense of how long this will take?"

"The initial survey shouldn't take too long. We can get the ultrasound equipment there soon and do a quick test and poke around the property. Depending on the results, we will know how much might be involved. If there's not much there, it could be as short as a few months. But if it is more extensive, it could take years."

"Shit," Paolo whispered to himself, clearly agitated by the whole process.

Frank said to him, "We'll need access to the property and the structures on it."

"I'll stay at least for the initial survey," Paolo said, glancing around the room distractedly. He scrutinized the students — young, attractive, idealistic, nerdy. He wondered if any might be gay, if someone might prove to be a pleasant distraction during an otherwise unpleasant ordeal. One male student — tall with tousled blond hair — stood out. Wiry and ascetic, he seemed unconcerned with convention. There was a raw masculinity to him that Paolo found appetizing. "Hmm," Paolo murmured to himself.

"Could we come out in three days, at the end of the week?" Frank asked, invading Paolo's mental ambulations.

"That would be great," Paolo agreed, relieved things were moving along. He gave Frank his card and added, "Here's my contact information. You can call or text the details."

"I look forward to seeing the property and the mosaic you discovered. Sometimes we uncover really important things by accident."

Paolo hoped it wouldn't be significant. He gave Frank an emotionless look and extended his hand. "See you at the end of the week."

Frank nodded and waved to Mauro, who had already begun to lead Paolo into the hallway.

"They seem eager to move things along," Mauro said to Paolo, hoping it might be taken as good news.

"I don't have a good feeling about this. I need to sell the property as soon as possible, and I have a feeling this is going to go on forever."

"Let's take it one step at a time," Mauro added.

Paolo hated that expression. He shook his head in disgust.

"Shall we take a tour?"

"If you don't mind, I'll just go back to Frascati."

"I do mind. You're not going back until you've seen one of the premier museums in the world. You need some cultural education." Mauro said.

"I need to work so I can pay for all of this shit your country is making me go through."

"You'll have plenty of time for work. Let's go."

Mauro grabbed Paolo's arm and led him forward. Paolo didn't like Mauro's bossy demeanor, but the feel of Mauro's hand on his bicep was oddly comforting. It had been ages since someone had touched him affectionately, and Mauro's grip piqued his curiosity.

They made their way through several corridors and rooms, eventually walking into a light-filled octagonal courtyard where some of the most important sculptures found during the Renaissance were displayed. Mauro removed his tie and stuffed it in a bag slung over his shoulder. He rolled up his sleeves. Although there were countless people milling about, suddenly Paolo found himself fixated on only one person, one body, who compared to the poorly dressed tourists, seemed exceptionally handsome. His dark hair glistened in the light streaming from above, and his eyes were deep, piercing, solicitous. Mauro smiled warmly and began an orientation. "During the Renaissance, Romans began excavating parts of the city with the idea of uncovering and showcasing the great monuments and art of ancient Rome. In 1506, this statue," he said as he pointed to a large piece, "was discovered in a vineyard. Michelangelo was present for its removal, and Pope Julius II brought it to the Vatican to add to his growing collection."

Paolo stood before the statue of Laocoön and his sons, Laocoön twisting in agony as serpents wrapped themselves around him. Mauro glanced over; Paolo's mouth was wide open in amazement. He hadn't seen him react to anything in Italy with any semblance of curiosity, wonder, amazement. It was an encouraging sign.

"This is one of the great sculptures of antiquity, demonstrating unparalleled artistic imagination and skill," Mauro continued.

Paolo felt himself stir as he contemplated the writhing muscular torso of Apollo's priest, a position not unlike a few he had witnessed after bringing home a hot trick. Laocoön's body stretched back as he fought the phallic-looking serpents attacking him. He found it surprising that such a homoerotic piece was prominently displayed in the Vatican.

"Did this inspire you to become an archaeologist?" Paolo inquired with a raised brow.

"Do I detect a little edge from our American visitor?" Mauro said, winking at him.

Paolo hoped Mauro hadn't detected his fascination with the carnal sculpture. He turned red.

They viewed the other statues in the courtyard, including Apollo — a figure with less sexual tension but nonetheless breathtaking in its poise and masculine composure. Then Mauro said, "Let's go down this hallway."

Paolo followed him, his eyes darting back and forth as he took in all the magnificence of the gallery. They entered a room filled with figures — some small, others large. In the center was a sizeable piece, around which people gathered.

"This is the famous Belvedere Torso, which was discovered toward the end of the 15th century. It made its way into the Vatican collection in the 16th century and inspired Michelangelo, as we will see in the Sistine Chapel."

Having seen the Laocoön just moments before, Paolo wondered if it was from a larger grouping. "Do historians know anything more about what it was part of?" he asked. He wanted to run his hands over the lifelike muscular thighs jutting forth.

"There are several theories – Hercules – since there appears to be an animal skin there – or Ajax, who may have been contemplating his suicide."

"There's so much force and power in the fragment. The entire piece must have been amazing."

Mauro was surprised at Paolo's comments and questions, suggesting a mounting interest and enthusiasm. "Yes. And it inspired later artists who sought to capture movement in paintings and sculpture."

Paolo nodded. He pivoted in place and admired the gallery. They wandered farther into another large, cavernous circular room. In niches around the space, there were towering larger-than-life statues. One caught Paolo's attention. "Wow!" he remarked as he stood spellbound in front of the piece. A tunic hung loosely from one shoulder of the individual, exposing a smooth and muscular torso, gleaming in the overhead light. The youthful face of the figure glanced down serenely, confidently, seductively.

Tears formed in Mauro's eyes. The magnificence of the works always moved him, but watching someone see them for the first time was emotional. Paolo had undeniably shifted from his ordinary apathetic self to one certifiably engrossed in the beauty surrounding him. "Yes, this one is magnificent," he said as he stood side-by-side with Paolo in front of the sculpture. He composed himself and continued, "It is a relatively late find, although it comes from ancient times. It is the depiction of Antinous as Dionysius or Osiris."

Paolo returned a confused look.

"Antinous was the lover of Emperor Hadrian. He drowned in the Nile. Hadrian deified him; made him a god."

"And this was known?"

"Oh, yes. Hadrian didn't conceal his affection for Antinous, and over the ages, the story has been celebrated rather than scorned."

"But this is inside the Vatican."

"Are you thinking they would object to Antinous being depicted as a god or to the fact that he was the emperor's male lover?"

Paolo scratched his cheek nervously. "I guess both."

"The Vatican collected all sorts of statuary depicting the gods and goddesses of ancient Rome — as you can see in this room alone. And as we will see in the Sistine Chapel, artists depicted Jesus and other saints in the form of these ancient deities. During the Renaissance, homosexuality wasn't the problem it became later in the Church. Many of the great artists were homosexual. Most of the popes had their own indiscretions — with men and women. Pope Julius, who had the Laocoön moved here, was rumored to have liked both sexes," Mauro concluded with a raised brow.

Paolo took a protracted look at Mauro, who seemed quite at ease talking about homosexuality.

Mauro, in turn, observed Paolo blush as he processed the information. He wasn't sure if Paolo was uncomfortable or felt exposed, that perhaps the discussion of homoerotic art hit too close to home. He hoped for the latter. Mauro took hold of Paolo's elbow to lead him forward. Paolo twisted his neck to take a final protracted look at Antinous, his mouth agape.

They proceeded through the galleries toward the Sistine Chapel, passing the corridor of maps and the gallery of tapestries. It was a busy day, but they arrived at the chapel during a relatively calm moment between large tourist groups. Mauro escorted Paolo into the room and said, "I'll let you take a moment. There's so much here to talk about, but first you must feel the impact."

Paolo gazed upward and pivoted in place, taking in the kaleidoscope of colors and forms. The vaulted space was filled with Biblical scenes, some Paolo recognized — such as the various days of creation, Adam and Eve, and Noah and the flood. Figures full of movement and color graced the niches. It was overwhelming and mesmerizing all-at-once, and he lowered his regard toward Mauro, his eyes filled with curiosity and humility.

"The ceiling is, of course, one of the greatest masterpieces of all time. The colors, perspectives, and scenes are magnificent. You've probably seen movies about its creation and the stories of Michelangelo's drama with the Pope. The Last Judgment, on the side wall, is in some respects more impressive, even if less well known. It was painted later in the 16ᵗʰ century, after the beginning of the Reformation. The mood of the times was more somber, as reflected in the themes of punishment and reward."

"And, as you mentioned earlier, I can see the incorporation of the Belvedere Torso and Apollo in the Christ figure," Paolo said proudly, looking up at Jesus in the Last Judgment.

"Yes, Michelangelo depicted Jesus in an idealized form. He is of stunning physical stature, and he has a regal, noble, divine countenance. He represents human and divine greatness."

Paolo walked up close to the wall and observed the various individuals being cast into hell and others rising up into heaven. "I feel the movement of the scene. It's alive, and I feel like I'm in it."

Mauro nodded, surprised again at Paolo's more engaged observations. Given Paolo's earlier lack of interest in even visiting the museum, he was amazed at the sudden shift. It was the first time Paolo had shown any appreciation for anything Italian. He resisted saying anything, fearful he might burst the fragile bubble that was forming. "Yes. Michelangelo wants us to be part of the drama of the final judgment, the moment when Christ appears, and justice is rendered. We are forced to consider our own character as we stand before the work."

Paolo continued to peer at the wall and contemplated his life, the weight of the choices and decisions he had made, and whether he was on the right or wrong side of things. He felt pangs of remorse for the antipathy he had maintained toward his grandfather and wondered why he hadn't been able to develop more of a generosity of spirit toward him.

He turned toward Mauro and said, "Thanks for bringing me here. I had no idea. Shall we continue?"

"There's one more thing I want you to see in the museum," Mauro said as he led them out of the chapel area and back toward the main entrance of the museum. Pushing their way through the chaotic crowd of visitors just inside the entrance, Mauro led Paolo into a quiet gallery, practically devoid of people.

"This is the Pio-Christian section of the museum. It's at the end of this hall that I want to show you something," Mauro said, placing his hand affectionately on Paolo's forearm. He pulled him forward.

"What are all of these?" Paolo inquired as they passed through a gallery full of magnificent marble sarcophagi.

"Perhaps one of the most important collections of ancient Christian art in the world. These come from the earliest centuries of Christianity, when it was finally gaining legal standing in the empire. Rich patrons had these carved with stories from the scriptures."

Mauro stopped at one of the large pieces and pointed to the rich marble decoration. "Here are the effigies of the buried couple surrounded by scenes of Jesus' miracles."

"The changing of water into wine, the multiplication of the loaves, the raising of Lazarus, the healing of the blind man," Paolo murmured as he recognized stories from the Bible.

"You're very observant."

"Is that a wand?" Paolo asked regarding the instrument Jesus used to perform the miracles.

"Hmm, good question. Some say it is a staff, although it is shorter than usual. Others believe it is a wand that conveys power, magical power."

"Like Jesus was a sorcerer?"

"Perhaps."

"So, did early Christians believe Jesus was a magician?"

"Most ancient religions ascribed to the view that holy people were wonder workers. Jesus wouldn't have gained much traction had there not been stories of miracles."

"But does that make Christianity a system of magic?"

"That's a complicated question. For centuries, the Church hunted down and persecuted witches and wizards. One could argue that Christianity was antithetical to magic. However, if you think about the rituals of the Church — such as initiation rites, anointing of the sick, the changing of bread and wine into the body and blood of Christ, the power of prayer to alter events, and the stories of miracles performed by saints — much of the popular life of the Church is about altering things through intention."

"Then why hunt down witches?"

"They threaten the spiritual privilege or monopoly of Church officials."

"As well as the fact that witches invoke demons, right?"

Mauro shook his head no. "Some did, but most simply used spells to enhance imagination or visualization. Magic is about intending something and creating the conditions for its realization – so-called natural magic. Think of the words magic and imagination. They are of the same root. It is about visualizing or imagining an outcome. Think of creation. God imagined light, the universe, creatures, human beings. God created human beings in God's image and likeness. Thus, human beings have the capacity to imagine, to create."

"Why don't we hear more about this?"

"In the early centuries, Christianity was an underground movement. It was considered a mystery religion, one that sought to help practitioners recognize that they were God. Irenaeus, one of the early Church leaders, said God became human so that humans might become God — or something like that."

"What happened?"

"Christianity was hijacked by Roman civilization. Once it became the official religion, it was used to concentrate power in institutional leaders."

"So, Jesus came to teach us we have power, and organized religion taught us the opposite."

"You might say that. Or, you could say that Jesus came to help us recognize our innate divine nature, and organized religion wanted to maintain control, suggesting that we needed brokers or intermediaries – the priests – to access God."

"Yet you are probably a devout Catholic, right?"

"I'm a man of contradictions."

Paolo raised a brow and stared at Mauro.

Mauro felt the intensity of Paolo's regard and added, "I like the rituals, traditions, the stories, and the art. As an archaeologist, I hope the excavation of the past will lead to a future that is more authentic."

"So, you are an archaeologist and a theologian!"

"I'm only qualified as an archaeologist. But the past can't help but raise questions about the present – religious or otherwise. But come on," he said, squeezing Paolo's upper arm and pulling him past other magnificent sarcophagi. "There are more pressing things I want to show you."

At the end of the hall, they approached a spacious semicircular space. They stood behind a railing. Below was a vast floor filled with magnificent larger-than-life mosaics of nude Roman athletes.

Mauro pointed to them and said, "These mosaics are from the Baths of Caracalla, one of the largest bathing complexes in ancient Rome. These are incredibly well-executed figures using tiny tiles or tesserae to create magnificent color and shading."

"They are stunning," Paolo remarked with his mouth wide open as he gazed at the muscular men with handsome faces and bold stances — many of them well-endowed and seemingly parading their personal attributes to intimidate opponents. The large expanse included many perfectly preserved life-size images as well as sections that were empty, areas of the original floor that must have been damaged and lost due to the ravages of time.

"These are considered some of the more striking examples of ancient Roman mosaics. The faces are not idealized, but are, in fact, actual portraits of famous athletes."

"You don't think there's something like this on my property, do you?" Paolo inquired excitedly.

"You never know," Mauro said, observing Paolo, who was practically salivating over the spectacle laid out before him. "We'll only know once the archaeologists begin to excavate."

Paolo shook his head. He hoped nothing significant would be found, that he could sell the property and move on. But as he peered down at the polychromatic bodies — imposing and seductive — he trembled. The faces and bodies arranged before him stirred something inside. These weren't just a series of lovely representations. They embodied a certain force and virility that he craved and feared.

He chuckled to himself as he surveyed the figures. He stood shoulder to shoulder with a man who, thirty years earlier, had the same complexion, face, hair, and composure. Mauro hadn't been as muscular, but he was every bit as alluring. He wondered what it must have been like when Romans strolled on the mosaic floor and brushed arms with naked athletes preparing for competition. He felt blood rush to his face and his heart pound forcefully in his chest. He pivoted slightly and stared at Mauro, who leaned over the railing.

Mauro turned, and their eyes connected. Paolo thought his legs would give way under him. "Amazing," he whispered.

Mauro swallowed nervously, realizing Paolo's hard shell was melting. He sensed there was a force within him ready to leap forth. He feared and hoped he might be Paolo's prey.

"Shall we?" Mauro suggested.

Paolo nodded pensively, and they returned to the entrance of the museum.

Once outside, Mauro asked, "I know you were eager to get back to Frascati, but would you like to grab a bite to eat?"

Paolo nodded. "Sure. I'm in no hurry."

Surprised, Mauro raised a brow and said, "I know a nice little restaurant nearby. Let's go this way," Mauro said as they made a turn and weaved through a maze of medieval streets. They arrived at a simple trattoria and walked inside. One of the waiters recognized Mauro, greeted him, and showed them a nice table. He brought them white wine and some bread.

"So, I still can't believe you had never been to the Vatican museums before."

Paolo turned red. He shook his head no.

"What did you think?"

"It's difficult to capture in words. The genius is unparalleled, and there is so much art in one place. It's unbelievable."

"All the years you came here, Carlo never brought you?"

"He tried, but I resisted."

"History and art are wasted on youth," Mauro noted with a chuckle.

"You must have appreciated things early on," Paolo interjected.

"Yes, and no. As Italians, we grow up surrounded by so much history and art. It seeps into our bones and becomes part of us. When I see someone experience a masterpiece for the first time, it is at that moment that I see the piece with fresh eyes and vicariously experience the emotions that take hold of the observer. Watching you see the Laocoön, Apollo, the Belvedere Torso, Hercules, Antinous, and the Sistine Chapel was moving. It brought tears to my eyes."

A handsome male waiter appeared at their table and asked what they wanted to order.

"I'll have a salad and *amatriciana*," Mauro replied without deliberation.

Paolo glanced up. The young man was every bit as handsome as Antinous or one of the athletes from the Baths of Caracalla. He had classic features — a well-proportioned body, a beautiful face with a graceful nose, dark curly hair, deep-set brown eyes, and a warm smile. "*Che cosa suggerisce?*" Paolo asked for suggestions.

Mauro gave Paolo a surprised look as he had, heretofore, given no indication of an interest in speaking Italian. He wondered what had changed. He took another look at the waiter and knew why.

Impatiently, the waiter said, "Everything is delicious. *Forse i rigatoni con sugo di carne.*"

"*Allora, lo prendo.*" Paolo decided to take the suggestion of rigatoni with meat sauce.

The waiter scribbled notes on a notepad. Paolo continued to scrutinize him, following him with his eyes as he walked away.

Mauro noticed. He was more and more convinced Paolo shared his inclination. He smiled contently.

Paolo turned back to Mauro and said, "This seems like a nice place."

"Hmm. Yes. The staff here are warm and friendly."

Paolo wanted to add, 'and handsome,' but held back, wanting to maintain appearances to Mauro. "Do you come here often?"

"Whenever I have business at the Vatican."

"That's amazing that you work there. Have you ever met the Pope?"

"Once, with a group of archaeologists who had done work on an early Christian site."

"What was that like?"

"It was Pope Benedict XVI. He was gracious and affable, but I didn't like his politics."

Paolo returned a puzzled look.

"He was very conservative. Pope Francis is so open and welcoming," Mauro suggested, wondering if Paolo might take the bait and reveal something of his own leanings.

Paolo knew it would have been the perfect time to say something to Mauro, but it felt as if by doing so he would be playing into Mauro's hand, putting himself in a position of vulnerability. Mauro had crossed the line many years ago, and he wasn't ready to let Mauro redeem himself with a nod to progressive papal stances.

"Hmm. Yes. I don't get much into papal politics."

"Do you go to church back home?"

"Since Carlo and Luisa passed, and my parents are ill, I haven't had much time," Paolo responded without much elaboration. "And you?"

"It's part of our culture. Anna, Emilia, and I still practice."

The information wasn't surprising and only confirmed Paolo's intuition to keep his personal life personal and private.

"So, are you involved in any digs at the moment?"

"No, I'm on a bit of a sabbatical. I have more of an administrative role."

"That must be nice."

Mauro looked off into the distance and didn't immediately respond. Then he said, "It gives me time to do other things. And you? How are you keeping up with work over here?"

"With tours of the Vatican Museums and site visits with archaeological teams, it's been rather challenging," Paolo said, half in jest and half seriously.

Mauro wasn't sure how to respond, so he asked, "So, what did you think of the museum?"

Paolo paused, as if deep in thought. The server brought their meals and poured them each a glass of house wine. When he left, Paolo said, "It was more than I had ever expected. I thought it would be another boring museum — paintings here, statues there, blah, blah, blah."

Mauro shook his head in disbelief.

Paolo continued. "The Sistine Chapel was both larger and smaller than I imagined."

"Yes. Most people have a similar experience. It's part of Michelangelo's genius — his ability to create space as he did."

"It was amazing. But I have to say that the ancient statues were what really moved me."

Mauro was surprised at Paolo's enthusiasm. "How so?"

"I don't know," he began, leaning his elbow on the table and pressing his hand into the side of his cheek. "I think it was the sensuality of it all. Perfectly sculpted bodies."

Mauro pondered what Paolo meant — whether the term sculpted referred to worked stone or to the perfect muscular male bodies displayed by the artists. He was more and more convinced of what appealed to Paolo and said, "It is all rather homoerotic."

Paolo turned beet red and glanced off evasively.

When he turned back to Mauro, Mauro smiled.

Paolo wondered if it was a sign of camaraderie or a sense of triumph, success at having managed to extract a fragment of Paolo's carefully concealed identity. He needed a quick comeback, and said, "I think I was taken aback by the impressive artistic skill."

"There's definitely that," Mauro conceded, but he knew he had ferreted out Paolo's story. "But even a perfectly executed sculpture does nothing if it doesn't capture the passion embedded in our bodies, the desires and fears that clamor to be released, to be expressed."

"You're probably right," Paolo stated matter-of-factly. He took a bite of his rigatoni. He now wished he had simply headed back to Frascati.

"When I look at the Laocoön or Michelangelo's David or the Dying Gaul and other pieces like that, it's evident that the artist comprehends, grasps, and expresses the inner thoughts and emotions of the figures. The artist helps us to see the interior landscape, the struggle with inner conflicts and competing loyalties. We all deal with them. Most of us keep them hidden. The artist pulls back the curtains and forces us to see ourselves differently; to see each other differently."

"That's too philosophical for me," Paolo interjected, hoping to halt Mauro's unambiguous attempt to lure Paolo into being more self-disclosive.

"Sorry. Sometimes I get like that. Must be an occupational hazard."

"I'm sure you must be an excellent guide."

"I enjoy it, particularly when the group I'm guiding is inquisitive and thirsty for more."

Paolo realized he wasn't curious or certainly didn't want to convey as much. He hastily finished his rigatoni and took a long sip of the wine, wanting to avoid any more disclosures to Mauro. Mauro picked up the clue, and he finished his meal as well.

"Well, thanks for the meeting with the archaeological team and the tour of the museum, Paolo said as a prelude to excusing himself.

"My pleasure," Mauro replied without elaboration. "So, will you be making your way back to Frascati?" he asked, glancing at his watch as if to convey some time constraint.

Paolo looked at his watch too, and said, "I'm afraid so. Lots of work."

Mauro got the attention of the waiter. Paolo reached forward and handed him a credit card, eager to repay the dinner Mauro had bought the other night. He didn't want to be indebted.

After settling the bill, they both stood and walked outdoors. The pedestrian side street was quiet as residents began to retire for the afternoon siesta. Paolo extended his hand and said, "Thanks for the tour and for arranging the meeting."

"My pleasure. Safe travels. I'll let you know when the archaeological team has some preliminary reports. In the meantime, if you would like to get together to visit or see other sites, let me know."

"Thanks," Paolo replied, although he was certain he wouldn't take him up on his offer.

"Well, *ciao*," Mauro said.

"*Ciao*," Paolo replied.

8

Chapter Eight – Glances

Over the next several days, the archaeological team did investigations of the property to determine what underlying structures might exist. Paolo worked from his hotel room and visited the villa from time to time to check on their progress.

Impressions of the visit to the Vatican Museums lingered with him. He couldn't quite put his finger on what had gotten under his skin. The art was amazing — vivid, sensual, and arousing. The writhing body of Laocoön, the seductive beauty of Antinous, the regal figure of Jesus presiding over the Last Judgment, and the haunting faces of the nude athletes from the Baths of Caracalla all stirred something in him. Currents that had been long dormant were flowing again.

Time spent with Mauro had been more pleasant than he had expected, and that intrigued him. He struggled to preserve a visceral dislike of him; one that began when they were teens, but which hadn't been revisited or tested over the years. Mauro's dreamy eyes, mellifluous voice, and enchanting smile began to melt Paolo's aversion. He found him affable, attractive, even a bit sexy.

At the end of the week, Paolo met Mauro, Angelo, and the archaeological team at the farm. They had completed the ground tests and wanted to present the findings. Frank stood just outside the cellar at a table with several rolls of paper in his hand. His students stood nearby. Paolo, Mauro, and Angelo gathered side-by-side, ready to hear what Frank had to share.

The gathering felt bizarre, incongruous with what should have been a simple pastoral scene — a barn door, a hillside covered in laurel bushes, and farm equipment parked on layers of hay. Paolo wondered if Carlo was looking down from heaven and chuckling at the sequence of events that now forced his grandson to slow down the sale of the estate. Paolo was not amused.

Frank cleared his throat and began, "There are some interesting results from the tests we made. It would appear that the underlying structures of interest are confined to the cellar area. We found no evidence of anything under the house or in other areas of the property."

Paolo sighed in relief. He smiled at Angelo, and he glanced over at Mauro, who looked exceptionally handsome — wearing a stylish pair of jeans, a form-fitting white polo shirt, and dark glasses.

"We did, however, find that the mosaic floor is rather extensive. It appears to stretch the entire length of the arched back part of the cellar and widens in the front of the cellar — in the barn area where the tractor and tools are kept. We will need to excavate, but we will not have to dismantle the vaulted ceiling or walls. We will have to move the wine vats, but we believe the floor roughly coincides with the contours of the cellar. Perhaps the cellar was an artificial grotto in ancient times. The composition of the stone walls and ceiling suggest that they are of ancient Roman origin and had been decorated at one time."

Paolo's face turned ashen. He realized the excavations would take time. He glanced at Mauro, who leaned forward and cleared his throat. "Frank, can your crew do the excavation? And if yes, how long do you think it will take?"

Paolo nodded to Mauro; grateful he had given voice to what he was thinking.

"We don't know what the condition of the ancient floor is. Sometimes they are relatively well supported by a substructure and can be easily excavated. In other cases, the mosaic pieces, the tesserae, are fragile and have to be extracted piece by piece. That is a long and tedious process."

"If not fragile, how long?" Paolo asked, hoping that the mosaic was well-supported.

"Several months or a year."

"And if fragile?"

"Years, depending on whether there are decorative elements worth preserving."

Paolo whispered to Angelo, "And what does this mean about the sale of the property?"

"Ask Mauro."

Paolo looked toward Mauro, who nodded as if waiting for Paolo's question. "What does all of this mean in terms of the sale of the property?"

"You can't sell it without getting permission from the government. And for the moment, we need to see what surfaces before permission is given. Since Frank doesn't believe the house is involved, we can permit the continued renovations."

Paolo gave Angelo a frightful look. "So, you're telling me we can continue the renovations, but not for any real purpose?"

Angelo cleared his throat and glanced at Mauro as if seeking confirmation. "The renovations need to take place, regardless.

Hopefully, even as the renovations are ongoing, we'll have a better sense of how marketable the house and land is or isn't and whether the authorities will prevent a sale or not."

Frank whispered in Mauro's ear, and Mauro said, "Paul, Frank and his team are prepared to start work next week. Is that okay with you?"

"Yes, please proceed at full speed!"

Angelo turned to Paolo and in a low voice asked, "Are you okay?"

"What can I do?"

"Not much. *Pazienza*, as we say."

Paolo hated the word. He didn't want to be patient. He wanted to make sure everyone was moving as fast as they could. He glared at Angelo.

Mauro exchanged words with Frank and then joined Angelo and Paolo. "Well, the news wasn't as bad as it could have been. You can continue with the renovations."

"Yes, but there's still a lot in the air. I'm not sure how much I want to put into the project if the cellar has to be dismantled or becomes state property," Paolo said.

"I have a feeling it won't have to be dismantled," Mauro noted. "And if it becomes state property, it is far enough away from the house that it shouldn't impact whatever you do to the house."

"Are you sure?" Paolo asked, furrowing his brow.

Mauro looked at the cellar and the house and then nodded. "There's plenty of distance between them. From what I've seen in other projects, there's no reason not to finish the house renovation."

Paolo gave Angelo a punishing stare. "We should have just covered the floor."

"I don't make the rules," Angelo said in defense.

"Spoken like a true lawyer," Paolo said as he rubbed his forehead as if under stress.

Angelo looked at his watch and said, "I have to go. I have an appointment in town." He walked toward his car, jumped in, and sped off down the gravel road.

Frank and his team poked around the cellar and pointed here and there, strategizing about how to best tackle the project. Soon, they squeezed into their van and left as well.

"Looks like it's just us," Paolo remarked as he observed Mauro scrolling through messages on his phone.

Mauro looked up and said, "Yes. I'm afraid I have an appointment in the city, too. I need to get going."

Paolo glanced over at the pool, the fresh water sparkling in the intense midday sun. Mauro had been thoughtful and caring during the exchange with the archaeological team, and Paolo didn't want to be alone. He found the pensive and enigmatic archaeologist surprisingly alluring and handsome, and he hoped to find out more about him. "Can I offer you a glass of wine?"

Mauro returned a surprised look. Paolo wasn't ordinarily gregarious or sociable. Given the delays he faced in selling the property, he imagined he would have been irritable.

"We could have a drink, take a swim, catch up."

"I'm hardly dressed for a swim," Mauro replied.

"I have spare trunks in the car. We can open some of Carlo's wine. The cellar needs to be emptied, anyway."

Mauro's eyes darted back and forth as if looking for a plausible excuse, but he found none. He feared Paolo was laying some kind of trap, but he hoped against all hope that perhaps a new Paolo was emerging. "I guess I can delay my meeting." In fact, he didn't have one.

"Good," Paolo said, walking toward the car to retrieve a couple of swimsuits from a bag. "This should fit you," he said as he held up a turquoise suit.

Mauro nodded and reached for it. He glanced around and realized the property was rather secluded. He opened his car door and began to disrobe behind it.

Without any attempt to conceal himself, Paolo removed his pullover and dropped his slacks, removing his shoes and socks underneath. He stepped out of his briefs and slid on white and blue striped trunks. The fresh grass under his feet felt comforting. He peered over as Mauro, facing away from him, was about to slide on his suit. The same buttocks he had observed thirty years ago gleamed in the Italian sunlight. But there was no Diana — only he and Mauro alone. His heart skipped a beat, and he felt his legs grow weak. He was no longer the naïve seventeen-year-old, confused and angry. He now knew what he wanted. He just wasn't sure if it was available.

Mauro tied the drawstring and turned toward Paolo, who said, "Shall we?"

Mauro nodded. As Paolo began to head for the pool, Mauro shouted, "The wine?"

"Oh, yes! I'll get a bottle."

"I'll come with."

They walked into the cellar and back into the area where Carlo stored his vintages. Mauro couldn't believe what the fates had orchestrated — he and Paolo were standing alone inside the intimate vaulted space wearing nothing but swimsuits. As Paolo leaned over the stack of bottles, Mauro took a long, furtive look at him. His caramel skin glowed in the soft light of the lantern, and although he wasn't particularly muscular or athletic, the contours of his back and the curvature of his buttocks were luscious, and he felt his desire mount. "Here's one. A blend," Paolo noted as he brushed off one of the dark green bottles and held it up.

There were a couple of glasses and a corkscrew on a nearby shelf. Paolo opened the bottle and poured them each a sip. Mauro lifted the glass to his nose, took several sniffs, and said, "Nice aroma." He took a sip and let the liquid sit on his tongue. "Hmm," he murmured. "Very drinkable."

Paolo observed Mauro breathe in the scent of the wine and lift the glass to his mouth. Mauro was in good shape. His chest had firm definition and covered in a light coat of dark hair. As Mauro leaned his head back, Paolo glanced down at the nice package pressing against the fabric of his suit, one he had observed excitedly long ago. "Nice. Let's take this," he said, chuckling to himself.

As they walked toward the pool, Mauro was incredulous and wondered what hidden agenda Paolo might have. It certainly couldn't be simply social. When they arrived at the deck, Paolo said, "Sorry, I don't have anything more comfortable for us to sit on. Does this ledge work?"

Mauro nodded.

They reclined on a low stone wall that bordered the deck and separated the pool area from an adjacent field. They both savored the sensation of the sun penetrating and warming their skin. They sipped the wine and let the cool, crisp liquid trickle down their throats.

"So, how are you doing?" Mauro began, glancing over at Paolo, who had just reclined on his back. He had crossed his legs and rested his hands on his chest.

"Frustrated. Angry. But what am I going to do?" Paolo replied, looking oddly at ease.

"You seem to be taking this better than I would have expected."

"I know. I'm a bitch."

"I didn't say that."

"But I am."

Mauro didn't know what to say next. He decided he had very little to lose and began timidly, "When we were younger, you didn't seem happy."

Paolo didn't answer at first. Mauro got nervous that he had overstepped. Then Paolo leaned up and took another sip of the wine. "I wasn't."

"Why?"

"I wanted to be home in Boston, hanging out with my friends who were at summer camp."

Mauro wasn't convinced that was the reason, and said, "I always feared you didn't like me."

"Hmm. No," Paolo began tentatively. "That wasn't the case."

"But you never spoke to me."

"You seemed busy," Paolo noted with a little resentment in his voice.

"With what?"

"All the girls clinging to you."

"I was annoyed with them. I thought that was obvious. I kept hoping you would engage me, rescue me from the torture."

Paolo chuckled. "I would have never guessed."

"Guessed what?"

"That you were annoyed. You seemed to enjoy their attention."

"I couldn't help that I was handsome," Mauro said, raising his brow playfully at Paolo.

Paolo took a handful of water from the pool and lobbed it at Mauro. "Conceited as ever."

"Hey! You were the conceit queen," Mauro said, wiping water from his chest.

Paolo cocked his head. Mauro's campy expression was not one he had expected, and it made him wonder if Mauro was, in fact, on his team. That would change everything.

"I was just keeping to myself."

"You were hiding behind your dark glasses and CD player. No one could penetrate your shell."

"And you?"

"And me, what?"

"You were inscrutable."

"Shy."

Paolo furrowed his brow in disbelief. Shy was not the word that came to his mind when he thought of Mauro. He asked, "What about Diana?"

"Diana who?"

"Diana Diana. She was always hanging onto you."

Mauro looked off into the distance. "Ah, yes. Diana. Why do you bring her up?"

"You seemed to have had a thing."

Mauro furrowed his brow. "I don't recall."

Paolo wanted to say, 'I did,' but he held back. Instead, he pulled himself up and jumped into the water, splashing Mauro in the process.

"*Cazzo!*" Mauro exclaimed, as Paolo surfaced.

"Come in. It's amazing."

Mauro still couldn't believe the new Paolo thrashing about in the water. He set his wineglass down and stepped toward the edge of the pool and jumped in.

"*Madonna! Che freddo,*" Mauro screamed as the cold water engulfed him.

"Sissy! It's not that cold."

Mauro treaded water quickly and forcefully, trying to warm up. He said, "I'm not like you cold New Englanders."

"I always liked this pool. It was my respite."

"All of us liked it. Your grandfather was so generous to invite us, and Luisa always made cookies and lemonade and other goodies. Those were good times!"

"Hmm," Paolo murmured, doing a few breaststrokes toward the other end of the pool.

"Not for you?" Mauro asked, realizing Paolo didn't agree.

Paolo shook his head. He looked sadly into Mauro's deep brown eyes. He wanted to cry. Years of pent-up regret and sadness were floating to the surface. With his grandparents' death, his parents' illnesses, the ordeal with the villa, he felt like he was having to let go of so much. He was floating in the pool in front of the man he had first lusted after and realized that, too, was part of his sadness and regret, having never expressed his affections and too frightened or proud to do so now.

Mauro swam up to him and could see the pain in Paolo's eyes. Paolo had always been distant, mysterious, and haughty. Vulnerable Paolo was novel, unanticipated, and terribly sexy — with his deep-set moist eyes and quivering lips.

Unable to trust his eyes and heart, Mauro held back. He needed more time before he jumped off his own cliff.

Thoughtfully, he said, "It must be doubly hard coming back and having to deal with all the complications of the estate."

"Yes."

"I hope the excavations won't be too onerous and problematic."

"Me too," Paolo noted. He kicked his feet off the bottom of the pool and floated on his back, gazing up into the bright blue Italian sky, letting all his worries drift away in the soothing water. Mauro's remarks about being annoyed with the antics of the girls when they were seventeen made him think. Had he missed a whole alternative narrative?

He kicked his feet and glided to one side of the pool, where he rested his head on the edge. He glanced up and Mauro was observing him. Their eyes connected, and each knew that their antipathy had thawed, even if only a little.

Mauro pulled himself out of the water and reclined on the stone ledge, closing his eyes and letting the sun warm him.

Paolo observed from the pool as Mauro's chest rose and fell with each breath. He watched drops of water slide down his luscious chest. He noted the way the loose fabric of the swimsuit rested on his cock. He swam toward Mauro, rested his arms on the side of the pool, and stared at him.

He visualized taking his finger and stroking the drops of water on Mauro's skin and then licking his finger. He felt ashamed of his thoughts, as if he were an intruder, someone transgressing Mauro and Anna's intimacy, their domain. Mauro's body belonged to someone else.

Mauro felt his regard and glanced down. He said, "It's so surreal. I feel like I'm going to hear Carlo or Luisa yell from the house or a bunch of noisy teens giggle and preen about. But it's quiet, and there's just you and I."

Paolo couldn't believe his ears. Mauro had given voice to the unfiltered intimacy of the moment, two lives frozen in the past and now thawing in the Italian sun. It terrified him. He had spent most of his life concealing his feelings from his grandparents and parents and others, hiding behind a façade of work and obligations. He needed to know more.

"Did you ever bring Anna to visit Carlo and Luisa?"

Mauro furrowed his brow and wondered what was behind Paolo's question. "Yes. Once. After Emilia was born."

"Carlo and Luisa must have been happy to see you," Paolo said. What he wanted to say was that Carlo must have been glad to see the perfect family, the holy family, one that Paolo didn't seem to be in a hurry to form.

"Oddly, they weren't."

Paolo got out of the pool and sat next to Mauro on the ledge. He took a sip of wine and leaned forward, waiting for elaboration. "*Come mai?* Why not?"

Mauro was again surprised at Paolo's sudden use of Italian. "I don't know. He didn't seem that excited. Maybe he wished it were you, not me."

"I could see that. But he loved you like a grandson, like the grandson he didn't have in me."

"I don't think so. He felt sorry for me because of my abusive stepfather."

"Hmm. I didn't realize your father was like that."

"Carlo never spoke ill of you. I found that strange, given how insolent you were."

"Insolent?"

Mauro held his hand up to his mouth as if he had said too much. "*Scusa!*"

"In all seriousness — and we'll get back to this notion of insolence later — I thought my grandfather was terribly disappointed in me."

"I don't think so."

Paolo looked off into the distance as if in thought.

"Did you and Carlo get together after that?"

"No. I didn't feel as though he wanted to maintain the connection."

"So, what's she like?"

"Anna?"

Paolo nodded.

"She's beautiful, thoughtful, inquisitive, and understanding."

"A saint, in other words."

"In my work, I had to be away a lot. She was very understanding of that. Other women would have been jealous or objected."

Paolo realized Mauro was quite handsome and that amongst archaeological colleagues, in various states of dress and undress, he would have been quite a catch — for men and for women. He raised his brow, contemplating the occupational hazards of camping out with young people in remote areas. "And?"

"And what?"

"Any indiscretions?"

Mauro wanted to say that the only indiscretion he had ever imagined having was right in front of him. He simply nodded no.

"Never? *Mai?*"

"*Mai.*"

"*Cazzo!*" Paolo exclaimed.

Mauro wondered if Paolo was surprised by his fidelity or dejected in realizing he might be unassailable.

"It's not that I never considered something, but the right person or occasion never presented itself. I'm not all that virtuous."

Paolo's heart skipped a beat. He wished he might be the right person and the right occasion. Could he seduce Mauro?

"She's lucky to have you," Paolo said.

"And you?"

"And me, what?"

"*Amore?*"

"I'm not sure I'm capable of love or romance."

"Deep down, you are. I'm certain."

"A few minutes ago, you thought I was insolent and conceited."

"That's a façade."

Paolo grinned. In fact, Mauro had nailed it.

"I'm waiting for the right person," Paolo remarked. He struggled with whether to stare at Mauro or not. He wanted and resented Mauro, and wasn't sure what he wanted to convey. He looked off evasively, then turned toward Mauro, giving him a protracted and intense look that left no doubt as to his curiosity and interest.

Mauro felt his heart leap out of his chest and worried his eyes might betray his own desire and interest. He lifted the wineglass to conceal his face and took a long sip. When he felt his face no longer divulged his sentiments, he glanced at his watch. "*Cazzo*, I need to get back to Rome."

"Sorry to have kept you," Paolo said with a surprised and disappointed look on his face.

Mauro rose abruptly and picked up his glass. He pivoted in place. "Not a problem. But I do need to go."

"Let me take that," Paolo said, taking Mauro's glass. Mauro's eyes darted back and forth guardedly. Paolo sensed Mauro's restlessness and haste to leave.

Mauro walked toward his car without saying a word. He quickly stripped off the suit and stepped into his pants and pulled on his shirt. Paolo had followed. Staring at Mauro, he wondered if his earlier glances had frightened him, had unnerved him in some way.

Glancing at his watch, Mauro shook his head. He was indeed late, and he worried Anna would be concerned about his delay. "Let's stay in touch."

Paolo nodded, scrutinizing Mauro, who remained unsettled, nervous. Mauro stepped into his car, clicked on the ignition, lowered the window, and said, "*Ciao*." He sped off, tossing gravel as his car traversed the driveway.

Paolo waved to Mauro and felt his chest grow heavy. It was 1995 all over again.

9

Chapter Nine – Memories

Paolo was alarmed by Mauro's hasty departure, worried he had frightened him off. He returned to his hotel, did some work, and then received a late-night call from Boston. The health aide reported that his mother had suffered a stroke, and his father was becoming increasingly disoriented. Both were at the hospital getting emergency care.

Paolo booked an early flight to Boston for the following day. Once home, he made his way immediately to the hospital where, after seeing his parents, a caring social worker met him and reviewed options.

"Your mother needs skilled nursing care, and your father is increasingly unable to organize and manage his life. I took the liberty of making some inquiries, and there's a facility that can take them both right away."

Paolo furrowed his brow. "They can't stay in their own home?"

"I'm afraid that would be difficult with the kind of care they need."

"Would they be together?"

The social worker nodded his head no. "They have different conditions and treatment needs."

"But I can't separate them. They've never been apart."

"I know. For many couples, this is a very challenging moment in their lives. If you can find some things that will remind them of home and of their lives together, that will help them to feel more at peace in their new surroundings."

Paolo looked off into the distance, pondering what he might retrieve from their home. He realized he now faced not only the liquidation of his grandfather's villa but most likely the dismantling of his parents' home, the one he grew up in. He would need funds from the sale of their house and even more to pay for their care.

The social worker made some calls to the facility and arranged for their transfer. Paolo made his way to their house, where he spent the night.

A week later, his parents were admitted to a skilled facility. His mother was in a single room where she could be monitored carefully and get physical and occupational therapy after her stroke. Paolo brought some framed photographs of the family to hang on the walls. Rita gazed at them as she clung tenaciously to a quilt he brought from their bed. Rita found it difficult to talk and grew agitated as each day progressed. Paolo found it disheartening to witness her decline.

His father was in the memory care section of the campus. Paolo brought his favorite recliner, side table, lamp, and bookcase. When he was coherent and had good recall, Enzo lamented his and Rita's situation. He was grateful that they were in the same facility and that Paolo visited frequently, but he realized they would never return home.

Paolo usually stopped to visit his parents on his way home from work. He checked with staff to see how they were doing and spent a little time with each. He usually saved the visit with his dad for last, never sure whether he was more or less coherent. During one visit, Paolo noticed his father thumbing through a picture album. He sat down on the sofa next to him and looked on.

His father seemed curious and asked many questions. He seemed more cognizant of people, places, and dates than usual. In one photograph, Paolo remarked, "That's when you and ma bought our home." Enzo and Rita stood proudly in front of a single-family house in one of Boston's suburbs.

"We were so happy," Enzo murmured. "You were on the way, and we knew we would need more space."

Paolo turned the page and smiled, realizing that most of that album documented his childhood. Rita had meticulously organized it with pictures of his baptism, birthdays, first bicycle, and milestones at school. There were family pictures of holidays, many of them of Christmas with his grandparents.

His father pointed to another album on the side table, and Paolo retrieved and opened it. Inside were images of Carlo's vineyard in Italy. Enzo's eyes widened with excitement. "Those were such happy times," he noted as Paolo squinted to make out people in some of the older photographs that had become faded and discolored.

"Who are all these people?"

Enzo leaned forward and ran his finger over the page. "Carlo and Luisa. Luisa's sister, Aurora, and her husband, Gianfranco. These were their kids. I don't remember their names," Enzo concluded.

Paolo recognized Joanna and murmured, "Hmm."

"And these were Luisa's cousins. They came from the Abruzzi to visit one summer."

"You remember all of that?" Paolo asked his father.

He nodded.

On the next page, there was a group shot of Carlo, Luisa, Enzo, Rita, and Paolo. Paolo realized he must have been five. It was a memorable trip, one of the first that he recalled with clarity. He had a new suitcase and had been eager to fly overseas. He recalled that during that trip, Carlo had let him drive the tractor. Paolo turned the page of the album and, sure enough, there was a photograph of him sitting proudly with his grandfather on the machine.

There were more views of the house, the barn, the garden, and the pool where he first learned to swim. Paolo observed his father smiling warmly at the archives of their journeys each year to Italy, the large dinners served on a string of make-shift tables, the harvest of grapes, time by the pool, trips into town to buy supplies, and the endless stream of visitors who posed playfully with Carlo and Luisa.

As Paolo flipped through the pages, the years progressed. He had become a teenager. It was apparent how the playfulness and carefree spirit of his childhood gave way to a more brooding adolescence. He furrowed his brow as he looked at group shots of his family — Carlo and Luisa stood proud, but Enzo and Rita gazed with concern at their son, who looked unhappy.

There were customary scenes of neighbors and relatives gathered around the pool, sipping wine and eating crusty Italian bread and local cheese. Paolo was about to turn the page when his father blocked him and pressed his hand firmly on the sheet of photographs. His father's face became red, and tears formed in his eyes.

"Papa, what's wrong?"

"*Guarda*. Look."

Paolo noticed a snapshot of a party by the pool. People were standing around a table filled with prosciutto, cheese, and fruit. Everyone had a drink in their hands.

Paolo looked up at his father. His eyes were swollen and his hand trembled. He pointed to Paolo, who was reclining on a chaise. Next to him was a handsome man.

Enzo pronounced his name slowly, pensively. "Sandro."

"*Chi è?* Who is he?"

"*Una cattiva persona.* A bad person."

Paolo focused on the man. He was young, perhaps in his thirties. He was leaning toward Paolo and smiled affably. He imagined they had shared some intriguing story or anecdote. Paolo searched his memory for a Sandro. "I don't remember him."

"Good," Enzo stated emphatically.

"Who was he?"

"A man from town. He did business with Carlo."

Paolo was surprised at his father's recall.

Paolo focused on the photo and on Sandro. He struggled to recall the man. He pulled the picture out of its sleeve and turned it over. Someone had scribbled 1993. He would have been 15.

"*Mi dispiace, figlio mio.* I'm sorry, son."

"Why?"

"You liked Sandro. We told him never to come back. Carlo was very agitated. You kept asking for him."

"I don't remember that."

Enzo shook his head. He was troubled.

"We didn't know."

"Know what?"

"That you were gay. Carlo was very worried. He wanted to protect you."

"From what?"

"From people like Sandro."

Paolo took a deep breath and realized what his father was trying to convey. He wanted to put his father's mind at ease. He said,

"Sandro was older. It was good for Carlo to protect me, to be concerned for me."

"He went too far. He made you feel bad."

"I don't remember that."

"You changed. You became withdrawn. You didn't want to go to Italy." Enzo began to sob, rubbing his eyes with his fingers.

Paolo reached his arm around his father, who trembled as he cried. Paolo looked off into the distance. He wasn't sure how Sandro's banishment changed his feelings toward Italy. He turned to his father, his eyes searching for more information.

Enzo kept shaking his head. Finally, he looked at his son and said, "You wanted to be with your friends, go to camp, join the swim team. Carlo feared you would go the wrong way, become *un frocio*, be gay."

"He couldn't prevent that."

"We know that now. But then, he thought he could stop things from happening."

"How?"

Enzo looked evasively away from his son. He cleared his throat and slowly said, "*Ragazze, ragazze, ragazze.*"

"Girls, girls, and girls. Yes, Carlo paraded them around all summer," Paolo acknowledged.

"He was determined to fix you up with a good Italian girl."

"So, it was intentional?"

Enzo nodded. "And the more uninterested you seemed, the more determined he became."

"How?"

"More parties, more girls, and lots of comments."

"Comments?"

"Your mother and I felt so bad. Carlo would make remarks about gay people. They were hurtful and uneducated comments. You don't remember?"

Paolo shook his head no. "I don't remember anything specific. I just remember being sad and angry."

"We have a way of suppressing hurtful things, painful memories," he said with a nervous laugh. "I've often wondered if my dementia is about avoiding troubling souvenirs in my life."

"You were always so understanding and accepting."

"Alone, with you. But with Carlo and Luisa, I am sure I didn't object to things Carlo said. Your grandfather was intimidating. I'm sorry if you thought I didn't love you as you were."

Paolo felt blood rush to his face. He realized that the anger and resentment he felt all his life wasn't unfounded, wasn't just a personality defect in himself. It was unexpressed anger at the hateful comments and innuendos that he must have been hearing. His grandfather had shamed him, undoubtedly in Italian, and his coping mechanism was to retreat into his music, books, and English.

Tears began to well up in Paolo's eyes. Years wasted in anger, regret, disdain. His heart had been filled with shame and self-doubt. Youth robbed of enthusiasm, curiosity, and wonder. He felt cheated by the very ones who should have encouraged and supported him.

He gazed at his father, clearly remorseful for what had transpired. He wanted to give him an embrace, tell him he understood and forgave him. But he couldn't. His father was an accomplice and couldn't just pivot at the end of his life and get a free pass.

"Your mother and I felt terrible. We could see the sadness in your face and the disdain you must have felt for our lives, for your grandparents' lives."

"How could I have not felt that?"

"We know. Can you forgive us?"

Paolo froze, emotionless before a father seeking peace at the end of his life.

Paolo gave him a tentative nod, one filled with restraint and ambivalence.

Tears filled Enzo's eyes. "We had a good life. Now you need to live your life. Be happy. Pursue the things that you love. Your mother and I will be okay."

Conflicted, Paolo said, "You can count on me, whatever you need."

"We need you to go find happiness."

Unsure that was possible, Paolo gave his father a tentative smile.

Winking at his son, Enzo said, "Go find a handsome man — maybe an Italian!"

Paolo chuckled reluctantly and said, "They're too complicated."

"*Si, veramente*," Enzo agreed.

"Me?" Paolo asked.

"No. Instead, you are wonderful — *un bravo ragazzo*. You were always so responsible. Be a little irresponsible. Let go. Have fun."

"*Non posso*. I can't."

"*Vai*. Go. Find love."

Paolo shook his head, not certain it was possible. He felt like his heart had been irretrievably scarred. He gave his father a perfunctory embrace and said, "I'll be back soon."

"*Ciao, figlio mio*."

"*Ciao, papa*."

Paolo returned to his apartment in the city, collapsed on the sofa, and sobbed uncontrollably. Anger and regret coursed through his body. He lamented the countless opportunities for love and intimacy he had pushed away out of his own self-loathing.

He had undoubtedly kept Mauro at a distance thirty years ago. Would things have unfolded differently had his grandfather not poisoned his sense of self? Or was Mauro hopelessly straight, and would he have rejected any overtures?

Despite multiple calls and texts, Mauro had been unresponsive since their last visit. Perhaps he had seen through his glances, had detected his desire, had fled in trepidation. He wondered if he had been offended — if Mauro's seemingly enlightened positions were all a show, an attempt to come off modern and open-minded. Perhaps deep down, he was a conventional Italian Catholic and regarded Paolo and his sexual orientation with disdain.

With the new information that his dad had shared, Paolo felt adrift in an ocean of indifference and antipathy. He had always thought he was defective, ill-disposed, someone who lacked enthusiasm or passion for life. He realized that the jovial five-year-old had been mystified as a teenager and had become unhappy and brooding. While it wasn't his fault, he wondered if he could ever crawl out of the deep pit he found himself in.

Mauro was the first man in a long time that had piqued his interest, made him feel alive, and stirred his body. In Mauro's presence, he felt his skin tighten, his pulse quicken, and his heart pound.

"Please, Mauro, respond!" he whispered to himself. "I beg of you — just one text, a few words. Don't cut me off. I'm sorry."

10

Chapter Ten – Unveiling

Paolo remained in Boston in July and into the early part of August. He supervised the ongoing care of his parents. His mother remained weak after her stroke and needed increased medical attention. His father had good and bad days. On good ones, he and Paolo went out to eat or took a walk in a nearby park. On bad days, Paolo sat with him and recounted stories from their past as a way to help his memory.

Paolo contemplated moving into his parents' house, making it his own. But the memories were not the most pleasant, and his parents needed money to cover their care. He sold their furniture in an estate sale and put the house on the market. It was snatched up quickly.

Angelo sent updates and photos of the renovation of the house and let him know that Frank and his students were making progress on the excavation. Mauro remained incommunicative, and Paolo quit reaching out. He had enough to deal with, so he retreated into the comfortable shell he had erected countless years ago.

One day, in early August, Angelo called.

"Paul, how are you doing?

"I'm hanging in there. My parents are in good hands, and their house sold. It's quite an ordeal."

"I can't imagine. I'm sorry the challenges with the villa and your parents' situation are both happening at the same time."

"Any news?"

"Well, that's why I'm calling. Edoardo and his crew have finished renovations on the house, and Frank is ready for you to see what they have uncovered."

"That's good news about the renovations. I can't wait to see them."

"I think you will be pleased."

"And what did Frank and his team find? Is it a big deal?"

"I'm not sure. He's tight-lipped about it. I look forward to seeing it, too. Can you fly over soon?"

"Hmm," Paolo began. He glanced at his calendar and said, "I could be there next week – on Thursday. Would that work?"

"Perfect. I'll let Frank know."

"We'll see you then."

"*Ciao.*"

The following week, Paolo boarded a flight for Rome with a layover in Paris. The flight from Boston was delayed, so he barely made the connection. In Rome, the car rental agent couldn't find his reservation. They eventually got things settled, and Paolo made his way to Frascati. Most Italians were on summer vacation, so the roadway was empty, and he made good time.

He drove up the driveway and parked his car near the cellar, where Frank and Angelo stood near a table covered in drawings and maps. Edoardo and his crew gathered nearby.

Everyone gasped as they watched Paolo get out of the car. He had dark circles under his eyes, his clothes were disheveled, and his hair was a mess.

Angelo gave him a frightful look and then put on his best smile, saying, "*Bentornato, Paolo*. How was your trip?"

"The same *merda* — delayed flights, lost reservations, and insufferable personnel!"

Anxiously, Paolo surveyed the front of the cellar and the nearby grounds, searching for Mauro. He presumed he would have been there to coordinate whatever information Frank had to share. His absence felt ominous, as if it confirmed Mauro's deliberate intention to put distance between them.

Angelo glanced at Frank and Edoardo with alarm at Paolo's apparent agitation. The meeting promised to be tense.

"Signor Minetti, we finished the renovations of the house," Edoardo began, hoping to start things on a positive note. "Want to see?"

Paolo glanced at Frank as if to ask his permission. Frank said, "Go ahead. My team has a few things to take care of before we show you the mosaic. When you are finished at the house, we will be ready."

Paolo nodded and followed Angelo and Edoardo to the house. "Wow. The façade of the house looks really nice — fresh paint, the window frames have been repointed, and the roof tiles are all in place. The landscaping is a nice touch," he remarked.

Edoardo looked at Angelo, who said, "I took the liberty of authorizing that. The terrain is so beautiful, but the house looked alone and sad. Now it is all tied together, making the house part of the beautiful property."

Edoardo smiled proudly and gestured for Paolo to come inside. Immediately, Paolo's eyes widened. "Oh, my God! Look at these floors!"

Edoardo sighed in relief. "Spend money. Make money."

"And these are porcelain tiles?" Paolo asked Angelo.

Angelo nodded.

"They look like marble. Potential buyers are going to like this!"

"Yes, they will," Angelo agreed.

They wandered into the dining room and kitchen area. Bright light streamed through the windows onto the stone countertops and the open shelving filled with Luisa's bowls and plates. "Hmm," Paolo began. "I like the look. It's modern and vintage at the same time."

"New sink. From Gino," Edoardo noted.

"Yes, I like the new sink. It ties everything together nicely." Paolo opened the new stainless-steel refrigerator and chuckled as he noticed a couple of Carlo's wine bottles chilling.

"*Ti piace?* You like?" Edoardo said as he watched Paolo scrutinize things.

"It looks amazing. The floors, cabinets, walls, and windows. It looks like new!"

"All go easy," Edoardo observed, suggesting that there weren't any surprises.

"Can I see the bedroom areas?"

"*Si. Andiamo.*"

They walked to the back of the house down a brightly lit hallway. "I love the new lights you installed."

"More light. Modern. New floors," Edoardo said, smiling proudly.

Paolo stuck his head inside his grandparents' room. His mouth opened wide in amazement. The space looked like a page out of a home and garden magazine with beautiful windows, stone architectural elements, a gleaming new floor, and the handsome oak bed. "Hmm. Incredible," Paolo said, smiling contentedly at Angelo, who sighed in relief.

They reviewed the rest of the house and then toured the herb garden and the refurbished deck around the pool with new landscaping and a brick oven and grill that Piero built. Paolo glanced across the way at the vines and noticed they had been trimmed and that the grapes were large and shiny. "Who took care of the vines? They were a mess when I left."

Edoardo explained, "Archaeology students. Wait for supplies. *Tempo*. Student know *vino e vendemmia*," Edoardo tried to explain in his broken English.

Angelo interjected, "One of the archaeology students grew up on a vineyard and knows all about winemaking. While they were waiting for supplies one week, she supervised the rest of the crew, who decided to do some work in the field."

"The tended vines should be a nice selling point for the property," Paolo suggested to Angelo.

"Indeed."

Paolo pivoted in place and took everything in — the umbrella pines shading the drive, the new landscaping, the rows of grapevines extending the length of the property, and groves of olive trees clustered here and there. He had to admit to himself that it looked nice and had a certain appeal.

"So, do you have any remaining projects?"

Edoardo replied, "Do you want more? If not, we are finished."

"It looks perfect. I'll settle accounts with Angelo."

Edoardo nodded and accompanied Paolo and Angelo back to the tent where Frank was waiting.

As they approached, Angelo inquired, "So, are you happy with how it turned out?" Angelo inquired.

"It's amazing. I don't remember it ever looking this nice."

"It will fetch a nice price. You'll be pleased."

Frank cleared his throat and said, "If you guys will follow me, I'd like to show you the progress of the excavation."

"I would have thought Mauro would have been here. Was he invited?" Paolo inquired of Angelo and Frank.

Frank glanced at Angelo, who looked at Paolo and said, "We reached out to him, but he's been detained with family matters in Bologna."

"Bologna? I thought his family was here in the Rome area."

"It's Anna's family."

"Ah," Paolo said without elaboration. He detected some hesitation regarding Mauro on Angelo's part and wondered if there was more to Mauro's absence that they weren't sharing.

"So, Paolo, let's walk to the back of the cellar and then proceed forward."

They walked on wooden planks that lined the center of the space. On either side, a beautiful mosaic stretched between the vaulted stone walls and ceiling.

Frank continued, "As you can see, this area is simple but elegant — an expanse of flooring with decorative edging and artistic images here and there — a vineyard motif. Undoubtedly, ancient Romans cultivated wine here, and this must have been part of someone's estate."

Paolo peered down at the surface. It had been cleaned, and it sparkled in the lights strung along the ceiling. "Can I?" Paolo asked as he reached toward the surface.

Frank nodded.

Paolo ran his hands over the surface and felt the irregularity of the tesserae or tile. The decorations were simple, but elegant and colorful.

"As you can see, the flooring aligns with the contours of the space and widens as we get to the front of the cellar or barn." Paolo glanced toward the front of the building and noticed tarps covering the surface. He wondered what was hidden.

"What's under the tarps? Can I see?"

Frank nodded and led him forward. As they approached the barn-like area in the front of the cellar, Frank leaned down and pulled back the canvas material.

Paolo leaned over the edge of the walkway and peered at the mosaic below. It included the same decorative vineyard pattern and a large image of Dionysius holding a juicy bunch of grapes.

"It's beautiful," Paolo remarked as he observed the almost life-size nude god celebrating the harvest.

Frank shook his head no. "Look over here," he began, pointing to the edge of the mosaic floor. "See the vines here?"

Paolo nodded.

"Look just beyond that point. What do you see?"

"The same pattern."

"But do they look the same?"

Paolo squinted his eyes and carefully observed the work below him. From his perspective, they were identical.

Frank squatted over the floor and aimed a wooden pointer at the work. "The art from here to the back of the space is made with smaller tesserae, tiles, consistent with higher quality work. From this point forward, the tesserae are larger and have less color gradation. It is cheaper quality work and dated later than the mosaic in the back of the cellar. Dionysius, while impressive, isn't consistent with what we would have found if the same artist who had done the back part had done the front."

Paolo recalled the impressive figures in the Vatican Museums, the athletes from the Baths of Caracalla. It was clear that the figure of Dionysius was not of the same expertise. "So, what does all of that mean?"

"The front part of the mosaic is newer and probably a copy or reproduction of something that existed earlier. We aren't sure yet how to date it. It might be as late as the 16th or 17th century."

"Does that mean it has less historical significance?"

Frank nodded.

Paolo wasn't sure whether to be disappointed or relieved. "So, is the site still of archaeological significance, or can we proceed with the sale of the house and cellar and showcase the mosaic floor as a nice curiosity and historical element?"

"The back of the cellar is ancient and of significance," Frank replied. He nodded to one of the students standing nearby, who handed Frank a rolled-up site map. Frank opened it and motioned for Paolo to approach.

"See these?" Frank asked as he pointed to several distortions on the electronic image.

Paolo nodded.

"We think that below this part of the mosaic, there are pieces of an earlier work. We think the original floor was damaged and buried or someone decided to bury it and build a facsimile over it. We want to excavate below this floor."

"How?"

"It's complicated. We can try to approach it from the side, but if that doesn't work, we have to carefully dismantle parts of the mosaic to go underneath."

Paolo began to calculate in his mind the delay this would invariably take. "What do you hope to accomplish?"

"If the original artist had depicted Dionysius like the newer copy, it's probably extraordinary, given what we see back here," Frank said, pointing to the back of the cellar. "It is worth trying to find the original pieces. They could be pieced together and might be quite impressive."

"I imagine this means a delay."

"I'm afraid so. We had hoped to finish the project soon. Now it will be more protracted."

"How does this implicate the house and the property?"

"We're still rather certain the cellar is the only structure on the property implicated. It will remain an active archaeological site for a while. With the government's permission, you can sell the house and vineyard, but the new owners will need to know this will remain a preserved archaeological monument."

Paolo looked at Angelo, who shrugged his shoulders. "I think Angelo and I have some things to discuss."

"I'm sure you do," Frank concurred.

"Keep me posted," Paolo said as he extended his hand to Frank. Paolo turned to Angelo and said, "*Andiamo*. We need to talk."

Angelo followed Paolo out of the cellar, and they stood under one of the large umbrella pines. "So, what can we do at this point?"

Angelo replied, "The house renovations are complete. Theoretically, you could put the house on the market and sell it as long as the state authorizes it. There would have to be a contingency attached to the archaeological dig. This might dissuade some buyers, particularly those who want an active vineyard."

"It is an active vineyard."

"Without a facility to make wine."

"Hmm," Paolo murmured. "How do we rectify that?"

"The only way would be to build another cellar or barn on another parcel of the property."

"*Cazzo!* More money. I can't. I've spent too much as it is. I'm through!"

"If you can carry the costs, it might be worth waiting for Frank to finish the excavations and then put the property on the market in the spring, when things sell quicker and for more money. By then, we will know more."

"Do you anticipate any additional costs for the house other than basic utilities?"

Angelo nodded no.

Paolo scratched his head and stroked his chin thoughtfully. "Everything is finished with the renovations, right?"

Angelo nodded.

"Could I move into the house while Frank continues his work, and we decide what to do next?"

Angelo raised a brow and replied, "You want to move in?"

"I just want a place to stay when I visit. A temporary arrangement. I've spent lots of money for a renovated villa. Why pay for a hotel when I have it to occupy? I could stay here from time to time when I visit. If I furnish it, it might fetch even more money, right?"

"I didn't think you liked it here."

"I don't. I mean, I didn't. It's growing on me in an odd sort of way. Don't get me wrong. I still want to unload it. But why not take advantage of the place in the meantime?"

"What about your parents?"

"They are in good hands, and their memory continues to decline. They recognize me less and less. I can work remotely. I could go back and forth between here and Boston."

Angelo nodded, then said, "Electricity and gas are connected and working. If you wanted to work from here, you would need the internet. We can have the local company hook that up easily enough."

"Do you have suggestions for places I could get new pots, pans, glasses, and furniture?"

"Sure. There are plenty of options here and in Rome."

"Well, let's do it. Let's make this a home!"

"Amazing," Angelo murmured, shaking his head in disbelief. "By the way, are you hungry?"

"I'm starved. The food on the plane is crap."

"Let's go. I know a nice place nearby."

They got into Angelo's car and sped off down the driveway and onto the winding road in front of the villa. Angelo was an aggressive driver, and there was little traffic. Soon, they were in front of a country trattoria shaded by pine trees and surrounded by a verdant garden of perennials and roses. The maître d' welcomed Angelo warmly and gave them an enviable table at the edge of the garden and under a nice awning. A light breeze cooled the terrace. Angelo ordered a local white wine, and Paolo began to review the menu.

"The mosaic is impressive, even if it is a later work," Paolo began as he looked up from the menu. Angelo poured them both a glass of wine.

"Yes, it's nice. It's unfortunate for you in terms of delays, but they may find some impressive pieces below the current floor."

"I have to say, in an odd sort of way, it's kind of exciting — like a hunt for hidden treasure."

Angelo looked at Paolo curiously. "I would have thought it would have made you more stressed."

"At first, it did. But now that my parents are settled, I don't have the same pressure to hurry up and settle things. Edoardo and his crew did such an amazing job on the house. It's a shame not to enjoy it for a while."

"I always got the feeling you didn't like it here."

"I don't."

"So, I'm confused."

Paolo wanted to admit that he was, too. He had conflicting feelings, surprising feelings, and he wasn't sure why. "It feels different."

"Why did you dislike things so much?"

"I don't know. It felt so stifling. My grandparents and parents kept waving a script in front of me — become an Italian, marry an Italian girl, have an Italian family. I couldn't stand it."

"So, now that they are gone, the pressure is less?"

"Maybe."

"Are you having second thoughts? If so, I have a lot of eligible women that I could introduce to you."

Paolo glanced into the distance. The waiter arrived and asked what they wanted to order. Relieved at the interruption, Paolo ordered a simple plate of spaghetti and tomato sauce with a side salad, and Angelo ordered ravioli with pesto and some grilled vegetables.

The waiter retreated, and Paolo asked, "Have you heard from Mauro?"

Angelo thought the juxtaposition of Paolo's question with his earlier suggestion about finding a local woman intriguing. He gave Paolo a closer look and muttered to himself, "Hmm." He continued, "Not really. There were a couple of administrative matters that had to be handled regarding the site and the renovations, but we handled them via email and text. As I mentioned, he had some family matters to tend to."

"Will he be back?"

"Not sure," Angelo replied, taking a sip of wine and scrutinizing Paolo more carefully.

"If you talk with him, let him know I am back."

"You have his contact information, don't you?" Angelo asked. "I'm sure he would be happy to hear from you."

"Hmm," Paolo said quietly, not sharing that Mauro hadn't replied to his texts or calls.

The waiter brought their lunches, which they devoured with abandon. Paolo was hungry from the long overnight flight, and Angelo always had a big appetite.

"So, you grew up in this area?" Paolo asked between bites of his pasta.

"Born and raised."

"Do you like it? I mean, have you ever thought of moving elsewhere?"

Angelo took a sip of wine and then said, "I always wanted to live in New York. I have cousins there, and I could get work. But my parents are here, and this is the world I know."

"And you knew Carlo?"

"Hmm, yes. He was quite a character."

"I know," Paolo said, chuckling.

"It was difficult to resist his overtures — his invitations and the invariable insistence that one remain after a party for another glass of wine or a smoke."

Paolo looked off into the distance.

Angelo noticed and interjected, "I take it you didn't have the best relationship with him."

Paolo shook his head no. "Don't get me wrong, Carlo and Luisa were wonderful. But it was hard. Carlo placed a lot of expectations on me."

"You turned out well."

"I disappointed him."

Angelo gave Paolo a curious look.

"I didn't marry and have Italian kids."

"As I said earlier, there's still time and lots of people I can introduce you to."

"Thanks," Paolo said without much enthusiasm. He twirled some spaghetti on his fork and savored the explosion of flavors in his mouth. He remained troubled by Mauro's absence and asked, "And you and Mauro grew up as friends here?"

"I don't know if you would have called us friends. We knew each other. I am older. Our careers crossed paths a few times, and our families knew each other. Why do you ask?"

"Oh, just curiosity. It's fascinating that we reconnected."

"Hmm," Angelo mumbled between bites of food. He remained intrigued by Paolo's interest in Mauro. He asked, "So, you and Mauro spent the summer together here?"

"Not really. He came to the villa a few times when I was here with my grandparents."

"Ahh," Angelo said, not convinced it was as unremarkable as Paolo tried to make it.

"Everyone must know each other here."

"Yes. That's a blessing and a curse," Angelo said with a grin. "You seem to have remained an enigma."

"I'm afraid so. My grandfather wasn't happy that I didn't visit. I had so much to do with school and work."

Angelo nodded as if he appreciated Paolo's challenges, but he didn't feel much sympathy for him.

"So, can you recommend some places for me to get furniture and household items?"

"Certainly. I'll text the information to you later. There are a few nice stores here in Frascati and some on the periphery of Rome. There are, of course, upscale places in Rome proper."

"Thanks. It will be nice to get settled. Where's a good market nearby? I need to stock up."

"Here's one," Angelo said, texting Paolo information and directions to a market. "In addition to food, they have some basic kitchen supplies — bowls, glassware, knives, and pans."

"Perfect," Paolo replied.

They soon finished lunch. Angelo dropped Paolo off at the villa. Paolo, in turn, drove to Frascati to do some shopping. Although he was tired from his flight, he was on a mission to get settled.

He followed Angelo's directions to a contemporary furniture store. Its inventory was exactly Paolo's style, and without much deliberation, he purchased a small dining table, chairs, and a comfortable living room set — a sofa, rug, two stuffed chairs, a side table, and a couple of lamps. He was surprised to learn they could deliver the furniture in the early evening.

He stopped at a nice market where he got basic provisions — flour, sugar, fruit, cereal, pasta, canned vegetables, coffee, and spices. The market included items for the kitchen, such as simple bowls, plates, glassware, knives, silverware, and a few small appliances. He packed them in his car and returned to the villa.

Back home, Paolo unpacked provisions and arranged other items in the cupboards. He was glad he had saved Luisa's sheets and towels. He washed them in the new washer Edoardo had installed, and later, made the bed.

The furniture store delivered the items later. The two hunky delivery men were friendly and helped Paolo place the larger items. After they left, Paolo took out a bottle of Carlo's wine, collapsed in one of the large comfortable chairs, and glanced around the room. An odd sensation overcame him.

The house seemed almost alive — as if it were a person, an entity, a being. It regarded him, observed him, scrutinized him as he settled into the living room. Paolo realized the house no longer jeered at him, nor did it provoke disdain or disgust. It was as if he and the house had achieved a sort of détente, perhaps even a degree of amity. It felt comforting. He smiled in amazement at the change.

11

Chapter Eleven – Remorse

"Thanks for meeting me here," Mauro said to Angelo as he glanced around the nearly empty restaurant located in a remote suburb of Rome. "I don't want to run into Paolo."

"I understand. His impertinence can be a pain!"

That wasn't the reason Mauro wanted to avoid him, but it was a plausible and convenient pretext.

"We should discuss the next steps for the excavation."

"Before we do that, how are you doing? I'm so sorry to hear about Anna's passing."

Mauro felt his hands tremble and his heart race.

"It's been a terrible couple of months," Mauro replied, and then he began to cry.

Angelo reached over and placed his hand on Mauro's. "How's Emilia?"

Mauro struggled to formulate a few words. He nodded. "She's okay."

"And you?"

Mauro continued to sob. He shook his head no. He was not doing well.

"We don't have to do this now. We can discuss things later when you feel better."

"No. We need to make some decisions." Mauro wiped tears from his eyes and took a sip of wine.

"Had Anna been ill for a while?"

Mauro looked off into the distance in a daze. He turned to Mauro, and more tears formed in his eyes.

"*È stata una lunga malattia* — it was a long illness. Heart issues." Mauro paused and then murmured, "She was so sad."

Angelo tilted his head to the side and asked, "How so?"

"*Non posso*," Mauro said, trembling. He couldn't talk about it.

Angelo knew it was important for Mauro to give expression to his grief and pressed him. "I'm sure fighting a long debilitating illness would make one sad and frustrated."

Mauro shook his head no. That wasn't the reason. "It was me."

"What do you mean?"

Mauro didn't speak at first. His head hung low over the table. Finally, looking up into Angelo's eyes, he said, "I didn't give her what she needed."

"We all fall short in one way or another."

"No. It was more serious."

All sorts of questions were racing through Angelo's head — had Mauro been unfaithful, was he impotent, had he been abusive or cold or distant? "You had to be away a lot, right?"

Mauro nodded. "But that wasn't the problem. In fact, it was a relief."

"Then what was the matter?"

He recalled the image of Anna slumped over the edge of the sofa that afternoon. Her eyes were red and swollen, and her mouth was quivering as if in pain. She barely had a pulse, and Mauro called emergency services.

"She knew."

"What?"

"*Non posso*. I can't."

"Mauro, I'm here for you. Tell me."

Slowly and in a feeble voice, Mauro began, "Remember when we met at Paolo's place to review the initial soundings of the property?"

Angelo nodded.

"I stayed."

"What do you mean?"

"Everyone left. I was there alone with Paolo. He insisted that I stay; that we share a glass of wine and sit by the pool."

"That's out of character for him, but go on."

"I shouldn't have. Anna was expecting me home. I let her down."

"If she was ill, whatever happened wasn't your fault!"

Mauro nodded. "She knew."

"Knew what?"

"That I betrayed her."

"With Paolo?"

"Yes, but it's not what you think."

"Then explain."

"I don't know how."

"Give it a shot," Angelo said as gestured to the waiter to give them more time.

Mauro remained quiet, deep in thought. Then he said, "I've never said this to anyone before." He wavered and thought he might lose his nerve. Then slowly and deliberately he said, "I wonder if I might be gay."

"Wow, Mauro! You? Why do you think that?"

Mauro's eyes turned red, and his hands began to shake nervously.

"Thoughts, desires, doubts, struggles."

"Have you wondered for a while?"

"Since I was a teen."

"But you married anyway?"

"I was never certain, and Anna got pregnant in Turkey. I thought I could make it work."

"I've been with you and Anna and Emilia before. You seemed like the perfect family."

"A façade."

"Indiscretions?"

"*Mai.*"

"Never?"

"Never."

"Then what's the problem?"

"She knew. She could sense it. She always seemed disappointed, sad, disheartened. Her heart condition grew worse, and we tried to extend her life as best we could."

"It's not your fault."

Mauro nodded yes.

"It was a medical condition," Angelo emphasized.

"It was an interpersonal one. And in the end, she felt the shift."

"What shift?"

"With Paolo."

"Man, I'm going to need more wine," Angelo said, waving to the waiter to bring another bottle. Mauro chuckled nervously.

Angelo continued, "Insolent, impatient, and angry Paolo? You have feelings for him?"

"I didn't think so. But seeing him after so many years brought a flood of emotions to the surface. I realized I had always been attracted to him, wished he would have glanced my way and affirmed an affinity of sorts when we were teens."

"Do you think he's gay?"

"He's forty-seven, unmarried, and has a roving eye. I could feel the intensity of his gaze that afternoon by the pool, and I savored it even though it frightened the hell out of me."

"Hmm," Angelo said with a sigh. "So, you never acted on your desires?"

Mauro nodded no.

"That must have been difficult and frustrating."

"You can't imagine."

"Then you have nothing to be guilty of regarding Anna. You were faithful to her."

"Sexually, but not emotionally."

"You did the best you could."

"But it wasn't enough. She died of a broken heart."

"If you think she knew, then she was an accomplice. She could have objected or challenged you or moved on to someone else. There must have been something about the relationship that worked for her."

Mauro stared at Angelo and realized he had never considered that before. He was convinced Anna knew or suspected or sensed that he was gay and that it was a disappointment. But Mauro was right. The relationship must have worked for her in some way. "What do you think that was?" Mauro asked Angelo.

"I don't know. It could be anything. You're handsome and smart and successful."

Mauro blushed.

Angelo continued. "Maybe she felt safe with you. If she had been abused before, you might have been a source of affection and stability without sexual pressure."

"But she was so sad and disappointed."

"You don't have to own that. You did what you could to love and support her and Emilia." Angelo paused, fidgeted with his napkin, looked off evasively, and then cleared his throat. "I'm hesitant to say what I'm about to say, but it may be important. You mentioned that Anna had been suffering for a long time."

Mauro nodded.

"Perhaps the timing of her passing coincided with your reconnecting with Paolo. Maybe she sensed that you were ready to embrace who you are, and she wanted to support you, get out of the way, let go."

Tears began to form in Mauro's eyes. He felt a great weight lift from him, one that he had been carrying for years. He felt Anna's love, not her disappointment.

"Are you okay?" Angelo continued.

"You can't imagine how helpful your words have been."

"It's difficult. These things are never easy. You are at a major crossroads in your life, filled with all sorts of emotions. Be easy on yourself."

Mauro nodded.

"So, what's next?" Angelo inquired thoughtfully.

"I haven't figured that out yet. We just buried Anna two weeks ago. I'm going to take some time off from work. I have a lot to think about."

"And Paolo?"

"And Paolo what?"

"If you like him and think he's gay, why not say something?"

"What if he's not gay, and it sets off one of his tantrums? Besides, I'm not sure I like him."

Angelo chuckled. "He is a bit of a challenge. But sounds like from what you've described, there's a good chance he's of the same persuasion. And I have to say, his demeanor has changed. He doesn't seem as angry or irritable. He's even staying at the house."

"You're kidding," Mauro remarked, raising his brows in surprise.

"No. I was caught off guard, too. The renovations are complete, and he said he would prefer to reside at the house rather than at a hotel. He bought furniture, pots and pans, food, and new clothing."

"Really?"

Angelo nodded. He watched Mauro's face change — his eyes cleared, his skin regained color, and a cautious smile began to form.

"Shall we order?"

Mauro, still deep in thought, said, "Sure."

Angelo waved down the waiter, and they each ordered a salad and pasta with meat sauce.

"Should we discuss next steps about the site?" Angelo suggested as they waited for their meals.

"That's what we came here for, right?"

"Maybe there were other reasons for our meeting, but we do need to deal with the practicalities of the property and the excavation. What have you decided?"

"I have been following the progress of the dig. So far, the discoveries are not that remarkable. The site is obviously historic. We can't return the cellar to its previous use. If the art were more impressive, a museum might want to add the grotto and floor to its collection. But at the moment, we want to leave it in situ. It will be a small satellite excavation that students and some tourists can visit from time to time."

"What does this mean for the sale of the villa?"

"The cellar area will no longer be part of Paolo's estate. It will come under the patrimony of the state. There is enough distance from the cellar to the house that it shouldn't be problematic to create some kind of barrier that separates the house and property from the archaeological site. People will need to be able to access the site on the road, but a nice fence or wall can be built so that there's minimal disruption to new owners."

"And what about the cellar and wine equipment?" Angelo asked.

"That's a challenge you, Paolo, or new owners face. Perhaps it's worth considering a new structure on another parcel of the land."

Angelo stroked his chin in thought and said, "Hmm. I'll have to give some thought to that and raise it with Paolo. He's not going to be excited about more costs."

Mauro didn't know if he felt sorry for Paolo or some under-the-surface glee.

The server returned with their meals, and they both took initial bites. "Hmm, delicious," Mauro noted.

Between bites, Angelo raised a question. "So, what are you going to do about Paolo? It sounds like there's unfinished business there."

"It's too soon. I couldn't," Mauro said, pushing some salad around nervously on his plate.

"Couldn't what? You don't have to sleep with him. Sound him out, share your insights, find out more about him. It's harmless."

"The thought of having a protracted conversation with Paolo seems intimidating. He's so easily provoked. It's unpleasant, and I don't need unpleasant at the moment."

Angelo chuckled and said, "Make it casual, professional, see what unfolds."

"What do you mean?"

"Arrange a meeting with Frank at the property. Tell him about Anna and see how he reacts."

Mauro took a bite of pasta and smiled. He washed the food down with a bit of wine and turned to Angelo. "I think I will call Frank and do just that."

"No harm in it," Angelo replied.

"You're right," Mauro said pensively.

They finished their meals. "Dessert? Coffee?" Angelo asked.

"No, I'm fine. I need to get back home."

"And I should get back to the office."

"Thanks for listening to me," Mauro said. "I appreciate your understanding."

"Years ago, I would have reacted differently, but we know so much more now. I can't imagine what you've been through."

"I should have come to terms with this a long time ago."

"We set our own pace, one that makes sense to us."

"I guess you're right."

"Well, if there's anything you need – even just someone to talk to – let me know."

"Thank you."

They paid the check and embraced each other before getting into their cars and heading off — Angelo to Frascati and Mauro to Rome. Once in Rome, Mauro emailed Frank and set up an on-site visit. He went to bed but couldn't fall asleep. Thoughts raced through his head.

12

Chapter Twelve – Puzzles

A few days later, Mauro drove up to the cellar, got out of the car, and shook hands with Frank. He hadn't alerted Paolo to his visit, hoping something casual might unfold.

Paolo observed them from the kitchen window. It had been two months since Mauro had left the villa in haste and hadn't responded to any of Paolo's calls or texts. He fought competing emotions of curiosity and anger. His heart raced as he considered his options. Anger won, and he remained inside, watching through the kitchen blinds.

As Mauro greeted Frank, he glanced over his shoulder, wondering if Paolo might appear. He feared Paolo would be angry, hostile, insufferable. He had reason to be with the delays in the excavations and his own lack of response to texts and calls. Yet he hoped he might stroll to the cellar and be friendly, civil.

"Come inside," Frank said as he led Mauro toward the barn. Frank opened the large wooden doors and walked toward a table set on a wooden platform. "Our patience has produced fruit. We found some rather significant fragments under the medieval floor.

It's like a puzzle trying to piece them together. This is what we have so far," he said, lifting a tarp.

Mauro gasped for breath as he realized the significance of what Frank and his team had discovered. He traced his finger over the partial figure. The quality of the art was astonishing. The thigh, buttocks, and back of a bather were depicted with rich gradations of color — browns, oranges, and yellows. Several other fragments were strategically arranged on the table, pieces that appeared to be feet, the back of a man's head, and some slivers of blue, perhaps from a pool. "These pieces are amazing."

"Yes. They rival the best of Roman mosaic art anywhere."

"Do you think there are enough other remnants in the ground to reconstruct a figure?"

"We hope so. With luck, the tesserae will still be attached to the flooring undersurface and not scattered in the soil."

"What do you think happened to the original?" Mauro inquired.

"Maybe there was an earthquake or some event that caused a collapse of the floor. Someone came along later, leveled the soil, and reconstructed the floor to align with the back of the grotto. They probably had no idea what was buried in the earth."

Mauro continued to gaze at the bather. His heart pounded rapidly, and he wasn't sure if it was excitement about the archaeological find or anticipation that Paolo might appear at any moment.

"What is the plan for continued work?" Mauro asked.

"We will continue to excavate. We think there is another figure. The newer floor has an image of Dionysius. But if the original had a bather, there must be someone else in the scene. It would be odd to have a single individual and not a counterpart. By the way, what have you decided to do with the site?"

"We will leave the grotto and floor in situ. The fragments of the original figure or figures will go to a local archaeological museum for display."

"How might this impact Paolo's sale of the property? I'm sure he is anxious to move on with things."

"The grotto will be under state control. But since only specialists will visit, it wouldn't be an active museum or something that disrupts the tranquility of the vineyard. How much more time do you anticipate digging?"

"If the tiles are intact, another month or so would be sufficient."

"I'll file a report."

"Keep me posted," Frank added. He extended his hand and shook Mauro's warmly.

Mauro walked back out onto the driveway and into the bright sunlight. The artwork Frank and his team uncovered was exceptional, and Mauro felt giddy at the prospect that a local museum might be able to showcase something so valuable. He scrolled through the images he had taken on his phone and compared them in his mind to the figures at the Vatican Museums. They were of analogous quality and shared a similar celebration of the male form — of strength, vitality, and seductiveness. He chuckled nervously at the fantasies racing through his head. He was tempted to knock on Paolo's door, but he lost his nerve. He had let too much time pass, and he feared the chasm between them had deepened. He glanced furtively toward the house and thought he saw Paolo retreat behind the kitchen window.

He jumped into his car and sped away.

Paolo waited until Mauro was out of sight and then sauntered toward the cellar.

"Oh, Paul. Mauro was just here. You missed him."

"I was taking care of some work. I didn't realize he was dropping by."

"He came to see the progress we've made. Do you want to see?"

Paolo nodded enthusiastically and approached the table.

"These are just fragments of a figure. We expect to find more and fit them together. But look!"

"Wow," Paolo remarked as he gazed at the beautiful art. "I can see now why you didn't think Dionysius was that impressive. This is astounding."

"Yes," Frank said proudly.

Paolo wanted to touch the tile, run his hand over the image, but it felt transgressive, as if caressing a real body. He stretched out his hand and then withdrew it, looking guardedly at Frank, hoping he hadn't detected his fascination or obsession with the bather.

"Go ahead. You can touch it."

Paolo nodded his head no. "That's okay. The quality is evident."

"We hope to find more remains in the ground below. Perhaps another person, too."

Paolo's eyes widened. "I'm sure you must be excited."

"We are."

"So, what did Mauro say about the site and its future?"

"They are going to leave it in situ. That means the cellar will be off-limits to future owners."

"I figured that was going to be the case."

"I hope you're not too disappointed."

Paolo rolled his eyes. "I'll have to figure out how to add a barn to the property in order to sell it. More money and time."

"The joys of foreign home ownership."

"I'm going to go back inside to work. Make yourself at home," Paolo said warmly.

"Thanks. I have a few things to do, and then I'm going to take off for the weekend. My crew is on a break."

"*Ciao,*" Paolo said.

"*Ciao,*" Frank added.

Paolo returned to the house. He logged onto his accounts to check balances. With the ongoing delay of sale, he had to make sure he could continue to carry the costs of maintaining the property. The sale of his parents' house helped, but he realized at some point he would have to sell Italy to keep up their care.

He glanced over at several photographs of his family. He still felt resentment that he was sitting in Italy, putting his life on hold, taking care of their unfinished business.

The image of Mauro speeding down the driveway after his visit with Frank flashed through his head. "What a prick," he murmured to himself. "He didn't have the decency to knock and say hello or text me that he was coming. *Vaffanculo* – fuck you!"

He looked up and surveyed the living room and the view out of the front window. He wanted to like it, to settle in, to embrace it, but as he looked at his accounts and mounting work back home, he didn't have the luxury to do so. He transferred some more investment funds into his checking account and then logged onto his work account and responded to emails from clients.

13

Chapter Thirteen – Coming Out

Mauro sat in a stuffed chair facing a large window in his living room. A gentle breeze cooled the room, but he felt clammy. His hands were sweating as he contemplated the call. He stood and walked toward the opening, glancing down at the historic street in front of his condominium. People passed below, strolling home from work or to the market. He gazed out over the rooftops of the historic center. St. Peter's Basilica loomed in the distance.

He pressed the number and heard the phone ring.

"*Pronto,*" Paolo responded.

"Paul, this is Mauro."

There was a long pause on the other end of the line. Mauro feared Paolo would hang up or shout some obscenity. Instead, he said, "Mauro. It's good to hear your voice. I hope you are okay."

Slowly, Mauro said, "I need to talk with you."

Paolo furrowed his brow and waited for elaboration. "What's wrong?"

"Can we talk in person? I have some things to share."

Paolo responded, "Sure. What do you have in mind?"

"Might you be free for lunch tomorrow? In Rome? Perhaps in the Piazza Rotonda, in front of the Pantheon?"

"That's fine. Is one o'clock okay?"

"Perfect. There's a place on the right side of the square as you face the temple. See you there."

Paolo paused. He wasn't sure whether to press Mauro for more information, perhaps a preview of their visit. He cleared his throat and asked, "Is something the matter?"

Mauro didn't respond at first. Paolo feared the worst — that Mauro was angry, or offended, or sick — or that perhaps there was something more problematic with the villa and the excavations.

"Nothing you need to worry about," Mauro finally verbalized.

"Is everything okay? Should I come today?"

"No, tomorrow is fine. Don't worry."

"Well, then. *A presto*," Paolo replied thoughtfully. He hung up.

The next day, Paolo boarded a train at the Frascati station. Although Mauro seemed preoccupied and concerned about something, Paolo was encouraged by his call and hoped they might get off to a better start. The ride into Rome was uneventful. The short trip had become familiar, and he blended in with the people commuting to Rome for work. At Termini, he navigated the chaotic throng of tourists and commuters rushing to and from trains, and he hailed a taxi in the massive square. In a few minutes, he was in the historical center and a short walk from the Pantheon.

He approached the restaurant and saw Mauro sitting at a table overlooking the square. Mauro stood and greeted Paolo warmly. He gave him an embrace and said, "*Ciao.* Thanks for coming."

Paolo scrutinized Mauro and took a seat next to him, both of them facing the square and the massive ancient monument.

Mauro's eyes were sullen and full of apprehension. His skin was pale, and his clothes wrinkled, as if he had been in them all night.

"Some wine?" Mauro offered, holding a cool bottle of white wine over Paolo's empty glass.

Paolo nodded.

They lifted their glasses and said, "Cheers."

Mauro looked out over the square, reluctant to look Paolo in the eye. He still wasn't sure how much he wanted to share with him, and he wondered if inviting him to lunch had been a mistake.

Paolo sensed his discomfort and said, "This is a nice place. Great spot to watch people and take in the sights."

"Hmm, yes," Mauro noted. "Oddly, I come here when I want to think. It gives me perspective."

Paolo nodded and said, "So, what's up?"

The server appeared just as Mauro was about to speak. "What would you like to eat?" Mauro inquired, relieved by the interruption. "They have all the classic Roman dishes."

"Perhaps an amatriciana and salad," Paolo replied.

"Sounds good. I think I'll have the same." Mauro ordered for them, and the server retreated.

"So," Paolo reiterated.

Mauro fidgeted with his napkin. After an uncomfortable delay, Mauro blurted out, "Anna has passed away."

Blood rushed to Paolo's face. He hadn't anticipated such shocking news. "Mauro, I'm so sorry. When did this happen? Had she been ill?"

"A few weeks ago. She had been sick for a while."

"How terrible. How come you didn't call? How are you doing?"

Tears filled Mauro's eyes. He shook his head, unable to pronounce a word.

Paolo said, "*Piano, piano*. Take your time. Breathe. Tell me all about it."

Mauro chuckled at Paolo's advice in Italian, wiping tears off his cheeks.

Paolo interjected, "How did she die?"

"Heart issues. She had been suffering for a long time."

"You never mentioned it."

"It didn't seem appropriate at the time."

"What happened?"

"She had a series of heart failures. They couldn't rectify things. She finally succumbed."

"How's your daughter?"

"Inconsolable. She blames me."

"Why?"

"Says I didn't do enough."

"How are you dealing with it all?"

Choked with emotion, Mauro simply shook his head.

The server arrived with their plates of pasta and salad. Paolo thrust his fork into the linguine covered in tomato, cheese, and bits of guanciale. He noticed Mauro seemed uninterested in eating. In fact, Mauro's stomach was in knots. Paolo hesitated to take a bite, but did.

Out of the blue, Mauro interjected, "I feel so guilty."

Paolo put his fork down and peered at Mauro, inviting him to elaborate. "What about?"

"I let her down?"

"Oh, Mauro, I'm sure you did everything you could to help her. It's never easy facing a terminal illness."

"It's not that. It's something else."

"What?"

"I don't know how to say this," Mauro began nervously. His legs felt weak, his hands began to tremble, and he was lightheaded. He could feel himself losing nerve.

"I didn't love her the way she deserved."

"We all do the best we can. None of us love as much as we wish we could," Paolo said thoughtfully.

"We should have never married," Mauro added.

"You must have loved each other."

"I thought so."

"What happened?"

"Anna got pregnant soon after we met. I thought we could make it work."

"You had a long marriage and a lovely daughter. It must have worked."

"She sensed it."

"Sensed what?" Paolo inquired, wondering if perhaps Mauro was about to come out to him. That might clarify the mixed signals during their last meeting and his precipitous departure.

Mauro wanted to blurt it out, get it off his chest, but he couldn't. He felt his hands sweat and his pulse race. To declare himself would be equivalent to declaring his affections for Paolo. It was his obsession with the insolent but handsome American, thirty years ago, that made him question his sexuality. He wasn't ready to concede so much so quickly. "She sensed that I was conflicted."

"About what?"

"About us," Mauro replied disingenuously. He couldn't come out.

Paolo swirled a forkful of pasta and put it in his mouth. Mauro continued to push his food around his plate, consuming a lot of wine instead.

"When we last spoke, you mentioned you hadn't had any affairs," Paolo noted.

"That's right."

"Then you have nothing to feel guilty about."

"But I do. She knew that I didn't love her deeply, passionately."

"How do you know?"

"I could see it on her face."

"You have to let that go."

"I can't. I keep visualizing it," Mauro said, recalling her weakened state when he arrived home late after being at Paolo's.

"I'm sorry. What can I do?"

Mauro paused. He recalled the moment by the pool earlier in the summer. He was certain Paolo had feelings for him. Would Paolo make his sentiments known again, or had he become dissuaded by his own hasty retreat and long silence?

"I don't know. It's odd — you and I. I feel like you are a friend, someone I've known all my life, someone I could confide in, seek advice from. Yet we are strangers, in fact."

"Yes, I've thought the same."

Mauro smiled warmly and finally took a bite of food. "I'm sorry for my silence."

"Given what you have been through, it makes sense."

"I'd like to get to know the mysterious American of thirty years ago."

"I'm afraid there's not much there," Paolo replied.

"That can't be true. You must have had all sorts of adventures."

Paolo nodded no. In fact, as he made a quick survey of his life, he realized that he had always lived on the fence, looking enviably at others, afraid to claim his rightful place. "I live a dull and uninspiring life — focused on charts, transactions, customers, and my parents' care."

"What do you do for fun?"

Paolo looked off into the distance. Mauro's question made him realize he didn't do things for fun; he didn't feel like he had the luxury to indulge himself. "Not much. I go out to eat or to the theater."

"You must have a nice circle of friends."

"Yeah, but we're all in the same boat," Paolo said, concealing the fact that he didn't have a lot of friends.

"For what it's worth, I'm glad we finally connected after so long."

"It is surprising, isn't it?"

"Indeed."

They continued to chat, eat, and enjoy the beautiful setting. After a couple of espressos, they paid their bill and stood, walking just outside the perimeter of the restaurant terrace.

"I have an idea," Mauro interjected. "I live nearby. I have a couple of books on Roman mosaics I could loan you as you follow the work on your property. We could have a drink and continue to visit."

Paolo raised a brow. He wondered if there was more to the invitation. "Sure. It would be nice to see your place."

"*Andiamo*," Mauro said, waving Paolo forward. "It's a short walk."

They took one of the side streets off the Piazza Rotonda, past a large coffee establishment. The smell of freshly roasted beans was intoxicating. Paolo watched as people pressed against one another to go inside and have an espresso. "It must be nice living in the city," Paolo remarked as they continued forward past several stylish clothing stores, small markets, and restaurants.

"Anna and I loved everything about Rome, and bought a condo early, when things were still affordable. It's nice having all of this at our disposal. What about you? Do you live in the city proper?"

"My parents are in a suburb, but I moved into the center. I have a small condo. Like you, I enjoy access to restaurants, shops, and other conveniences."

"This way," Mauro said, as he gestured for Paolo to follow him. The road became little more than a space between buildings. Paolo glanced up at the sliver of blue sky and countless balconies crowded with potted plants hanging overhead. They needled their way through Vespas chained to light poles and over uneven cobblestone pavement to an unremarkable blue-lacquered wooden door set in a stone door frame.

Mauro led them into a small courtyard filled with potted geraniums. They climbed a narrow staircase and entered the top-floor condo.

"Wow!" Paolo remarked as he walked into the room.

"Hmm," Mauro murmured. "We were able to take down some walls, creating a nice spacious living area. We were immediately drawn to the large windows and light."

"It's amazing," Paolo said, pivoting in place. He glanced up at the wood-beamed ceiling, the handsomely stained plaster walls, the antique floor, Persian carpets, and the comfortable contemporary furniture. He walked to one of the walls and peered at several original oil paintings. "I see your love of archaeology carries over into the choice of paintings."

"Yes. Anna and I both love the artist. He specializes in luminous depictions of archaeological sites."

"Impressive."

"A drink?" Mauro offered.

"What do you have?"

"What would you like?"

Paolo chuckled at the thoughts racing through his head. He wanted Mauro. "I'll have a Campari and soda, if that's okay."

"Perfect."

Mauro approached a credenza, pulled out two glasses, retreated to the kitchen for ice, and then mixed their drinks. "*Voila.*"

"*Grazie.* Cheers," Paolo said.

"Let me show you the books I want to loan you," Mauro said, approaching a case filled with all sorts of works on art, history, and archaeology. He ran his finger over the bindings and pulled one out. "This one should be a good overview of Roman mosaics with nice photos of some of the more impressive pieces. Shall we?" Mauro suggested, as he pointed to the sofa.

They both sat side by side on the edge of the cushion as Mauro began to flip through the book. Paolo could feel intense heat emanating from Mauro's body and breathed in his distinctive scent — an earthy and sweet aroma.

"I never asked. What's your specialty in archaeology?"

"Etruscan excavations."

Paolo gave him a curious look.

"The Etruscans predated the Romans. They were astute in the arts of divination?"

"What?"

"Telling the future. Reading the signs. Figuring out what was going on below the surface, things that might shape the course of events. That's why the Roman Senate was built as a temple, and every decision included a consultation with the auguries."

"And Roman mosaics?"

"Well, they are always visually stimulating, as you can see here," he said as he opened the book to the reproductions of the figures from the Baths of Caracalla.

"We saw these."

"Yes. And from what Frank has shown me, the mosaic on your property is equally impressive."

Paolo scrutinized the images — remarkable nude athletes. He blushed. He turned toward Mauro and glanced at him. He shared the same features — the dark complexion, broad forehead, dark hair, and muscular frame. Paolo brushed his hand against Mauro's as he pointed to one of the figures. "You think something like this will be pieced together?"

Mauro felt his legs go weak. He knew what he wanted to do, who he wanted to touch. He placed his hand on Paolo's thigh and said, "Frank seems to think so."

Paolo felt bolts of energy pass up his leg and into his chest. Mauro's hand was warm, and his eyes were filled with tenderness and longing. Paolo leaned toward him, and in a soft seductive voice said, "It's kind of exciting." He reached over and turned the page, resting his hand next to Mauro's.

The gesture wasn't wasted on Mauro, who felt Paolo's mounting curiosity. The ball was in his court. He needed to make a move. Throwing all caution to the wind, he leaned toward Paolo and gave him a kiss.

Paolo recoiled at first, peered into Mauro's eyes, and nodded. He then kissed him back, surrounding Mauro's luscious lips with his own. He breathed Mauro in and ran his hands over Mauro's shoulders.

Mauro dropped the book on the floor and leaned into Paolo. He was about to say something, and Paolo put his finger up to his mouth and said, "Shh."

Paolo ran his fingers over Mauro's brow. He had always hoped Mauro would see him, recognize him for who he was, affirm some kind of affinity. Paolo kissed Mauro's eyes, wetting his dark lashes.

"*Madonna. Quanto sei bello* – how handsome you are," Mauro said as he peered into Paolo's eyes.

Paolo didn't feel handsome. But Mauro's words eased his self-doubts, and he felt his desire for Mauro intensify. He was uncertain how far he might be able to go, how comfortable Mauro might be.

"*Inaspettato* – totally unexpected," Paolo whispered as he slid his hand up under Mauro's polo shirt. Mauro's skin was hot, and Paolo could feel Mauro's muscles tighten with arousal. Paolo gazed into Mauro's eyes as if to ask permission, to confirm he was okay.

Mauro ran his hands along Paolo's thigh and in between his legs, grazing the edges of Paolo's balls. "*Cazzo*," Paolo said as Mauro explored his firmness.

Both knew they were at a crossroads, and both feared they would retreat. Paolo took the lead and began to unbuckle Mauro's belt and unzip his pants. He took hold of Mauro's cock as it sprung free of the undershorts. He stroked Mauro, who leaned back, moaned, and savored the feel of Paolo's hands on his flesh. All his life, he had longed for a man to take hold of him. The fact that it was Paolo made his body tremble.

Paolo felt an odd sensation overcome him. He now knew Mauro's secret. Mauro was in his hands, in his power. He could bring Mauro to his knees, bring him to beg for more. He began to stroke him firmly, and he watched Mauro writhe in pleasure.

Paolo slowed his pace and watched Mauro's eyes open, longing for him to continue. Paolo let him go and leaned back, unzipping his own pants and pulling out his formidable erection. Mauro's eyes widened in amazement. He was hungry, ravenous, and wanted to consume Paolo. He leaned over and instinctively took Paolo in his mouth, bathing him in hot saliva. Paolo screamed, "Oh fuck," as Mauro began to work him.

Paolo was almost at the point of coming when Mauro leaned back. He took his own cock and began to stroke it. Paolo took his, and together they faced each other. Each gazed at the object of their teenage infatuation, recalling in detail the features that had intrigued them, stirred them, gripped them. They stared at each other, cognizant of the melting shells they had erected years before. They worked themselves feverishly, feeling their bodies stiffen with arousal and then explode in a pounding climax. They both fell backwards, panting heavily.

After a long pause, Paolo leaned forward and whispered to Mauro, "So, you are conflicted?"

"Hmm, guess not," Mauro replied with a grin on his face, gazing into Paolo's intense brown eyes.

"I should say not."

"And you?" Mauro inquired.

"Do I look conflicted?"

Mauro nodded no. He paused and then said, "Thirty years ago?"

"What?"

"Why didn't we make the connection, then?" Mauro asked.

"I didn't like you," Paolo said emphatically.

"I didn't like you either," Mauro replied.

Both chuckled.

"And now?" Mauro pressed.

"To be determined."

"Always aloof."

"That's my middle name," Paolo noted. He slid to the edge of the sofa and zipped up his pants. He stood and took hold of the book. "Thanks for the book. I look forward to reading it."

Mauro raised a brow, unnerved that Paolo looked like he was about to excuse himself. "Stay. We can talk."

"I need to get back to the villa. Let's stay in touch," he said.

"Just another drink," Mauro implored, wondering why, after their exchange, Paolo seemed eager to leave.

Paolo looked off pensively, considering Mauro's invitation. He was tempted, but he wasn't ready for an extended intimate time together. Too much might be stirred up. He needed to preserve detachment, and he felt his resolve wavering. "I wish I could, but I really need to get home."

Mauro stood, adjusted himself, zipped up his pants, and leaned toward Paolo, giving him a kiss.

Paolo kissed him back enthusiastically and gave Mauro an intense look as he pulled away.

"I'm sorry to hear about Anna," Paolo said, recalling the original reason for their meeting. "I hope you will be okay."

"I will."

Paolo gave Mauro an embrace, one that was warm yet dismissive. He walked toward the front door of the apartment and let himself out. He hailed a taxi on the Corso and headed to Termini, where he caught a train back to Frascati.

In the carriage, he thumbed through the book Mauro had given him, hoping the pages of text and images might distract him from the troubling emotions coursing through his body. He berated himself for having given in to his teenage fantasies, for indulging himself with Mauro. He realized he had created a mess — had probably ignited hopes and expectations in a vulnerable person coming out late in life. He had always fantasized about Mauro, and their exchange had been gratifying, but it made extracting himself from Italy all-the-more complicated and challenging. He sighed as he calculated the costs of what had just transpired.

Mauro collapsed back onto the sofa, shaking his head in disbelief. In his wildest imagination, he would never have considered such an exchange between them possible. He smiled contently, then he furrowed his brow, uncertain of Paolo's sentiments. It was clear he was gay, and there was definitely chemistry between them, but Paolo had held back and had been restrained in their farewell. He remained a riddle and a puzzle, one Mauro was determined to solve.

14

Chapter Fourteen – A New Cellar

"*Ciao, Angelo,*" Paolo responded as he saw his name on the phone.

"Paolo, I have some news I'd like to discuss with you. Are you home?"

"Yeah. Sure. Come on over."

A short while later, Angelo drove up the driveway and knocked on Paolo's door.

"*Avanti,*" Paolo said as he invited Angelo inside.

"Wow! I love how you've decorated things," Angelo said as he marveled at the new furniture and art.

"It's come together. I am enjoying it, but I also hope what I've done will appeal to new buyers."

"It will," Angelo said. "But about that."

"What?" Paolo asked with alarm.

"As you know, your cellar will be part of the archaeological patrimony of Italy. If you want to sell the property as an active vineyard, with a wine vat and cellar, we need to come up with a solution. Well, I think we might have one," he said gleefully.

"I'm intrigued."

"Your neighbor, Signor Cipro, is older. He no longer wants to make wine. A local company wants to lease his land, but they don't need the cellar."

"I'm not sure I am making the connection."

"Signor Cipro is willing to sell you his cellar at a good price."

"I don't want to spend anymore money."

"It will be to your advantage when you try to sell."

"I don't care."

With a disappointed look, Angelo said, "At least let's take a look. The cellar is adjacent to your property. New buyers would think it was always part of the original estate."

Paolo looked at his watch. He had been working all morning. "I guess I could take a break."

Angelo dangled some keys in front of him. "*Andiamo?*"

They walked outside and noticed a car speeding up the driveway. The driver got out. It was Mauro.

Angelo and Paolo looked at each other. "Were you expecting Mauro?" Angelo asked.

"No. Were you?"

"No."

They both approached Mauro.

"Mauro," Angelo said excitedly, extending his hand. Mauro nodded to him.

"Paolo," Mauro said, glancing back and forth between Angelo and Paolo. He had hoped to have Paolo to himself.

Angelo looked at them both, detecting an awkward narrative under the surface. "What brings you to Frascati?" Angelo asked.

"I have a meeting with Frank. We are discussing final plans for the site, and I want to see more of what they have uncovered," he replied, making up a pretext quickly.

"Well, we don't want to get in your way," Paolo said.

"Mauro, do you have a second?" Angelo interjected. "I think we have a solution to the problem of the cellar. The neighbor wants to sell Paul his cellar. Come, take a look."

Mauro hesitated and glanced at Paolo. Paolo stared at Mauro, giving him a stern look as if to dissuade him.

"Come on. Let's see what's there," Angelo pressed, waving them both forward. "It's only a short walk over the ridge to Cipro's land and his cellar."

As they reached the top of the hill, Paolo looked down. Cipro had a barn, a greenhouse, and a subterranean cellar, just like Carlo's. They walked toward the cluster of buildings.

"The barn is in good shape," Angelo noted. "It's nice in that it's a separate structure. You can keep the tractor and other equipment there." He gestured for Paolo and Mauro to follow him, and they walked inside the cellar itself. "The wine equipment is older, according to Cipro. Since Carlo's is in good shape, you can place your equipment here and sell Cipro's," Angelo explained.

Paolo smiled as they explored the space. It was larger than Carlo's, with double the number of barrels and wine racks. The space was cool and had a nice stone floor extending deep inside the hill.

"No ancient Roman mosaics?" Paolo asked sarcastically.

"As long as the floor remains intact, we'll never know," Mauro observed, grinning.

Paolo blushed, then he said, "It's nice, but I don't want any more outlays. I told you I'm through!"

"I know," Angelo replied. "But it's a strategic move, one that will net more return on what you've already spent."

"I keep spending, but there's no return."

Angelo glanced at Mauro and gave him a frightful look. Paolo seemed exceptionally irritable. Angelo hoped Mauro might chime in. He didn't.

"How much does he want?" Paolo asked.

Angelo pulled a prospectus out of his jacket and handed it to him. "It seems like a fair offer."

Paolo studied the document. The cost was less than he anticipated, but he was still annoyed at all the expenses and delays. "Hmm," he said. "It doesn't seem that costly. Would he be willing to sell it contingent on the sale of my property?"

"That's an intriguing idea. Although I think he was excited to learn you were back, that you might carry on Carlo's legacy."

"Who gave him that idea?" Paolo interjected angrily.

Angelo looked off evasively. "No one. I think he inferred it."

"Let me think about it."

"Don't take too long. He might find another buyer."

"I'll be back in touch shortly."

Angelo nodded. The three of them walked back up the hill and onto Paolo's property.

"Well, I have to get back to the office. Give me a call," Angelo said, extending his hand to Paolo. He gave Mauro a protracted look, hoping he might disclose something in his eyes.

Mauro sensed Angelo's curiosity, put on a good poker face, and said, "A pleasant surprise to see you, Angelo. Let me speak with Frank, and I will be in touch with more details about the site."

Mauro and Angelo shook hands, and Angelo got into his car and sped off.

Paolo said, "When you are through with Frank, come have a drink."

Mauro winked at Paolo and walked toward the cellar.

A half-hour later, Mauro walked up to Paolo's back door and knocked.

"*Avanti* – come in," Paolo yelled from inside.

Mauro entered and leaned in to give Paolo a kiss on his mouth, but Paolo turned to give him his cheek. "The neighbors," he said half-jokingly, half-seriously. He could see Frank from the doorway and didn't want problems.

"Something to drink?" Paolo offered.

"Some water, thanks."

Paolo poured them each a glass of water and led them into the living room where, during an awkwardly long silent pause, they sat on the sofa and Paolo said, "So, here we are."

"Hmm," Mauro murmured, fearful that he had presumed upon Paolo's interest. "Thanks for the talk yesterday. It helped."

"Anytime."

"I'm sorry if I was presumptuous."

"No. You weren't. It was probably a long time in the making," Paolo said, blushing. He still wasn't sure how much he wanted to encourage Mauro.

"It's all so surreal."

"I know," Paolo admitted.

Mauro glanced around the room nervously. He spotted the box of photos Paolo had on one of the side tables. "What are those?"

"Old pictures. I found them cleaning out the house."

"Anything interesting?"

Paolo stood and reached for them. He rummaged through the photographs and then pulled out the one of the two of them. He rubbed his fingers over it and handed it to Mauro. "What do you think?"

"Wow! What a picture!" Mauro said in disbelief as he scrutinized the image. "Look at us!"

"Yes. We were young."

"And sexy!" Mauro noted. Mauro gazed at the two of them. Paolo was looking away, sad, pensive. "You didn't like me, did you?"

"I didn't like myself."

"Why not?"

"I thought I was just uninteresting, unfriendly – *antipatico* as everyone called me."

"And?"

"I had a conversation with my dad when I was back in Boston. I came to find out that Carlo feared I might be gay and was doing everything in his power to shame me into being straight."

Mauro looked at him quizzically.

"Innuendos, slurs — you know, about gay people. I was naïve and not self-aware. I guess I internalized the messages and thought there was something horribly wrong with me."

"That's terrible."

"Yes. If someone says something often enough, you begin to believe them — particularly if it is your grandfather."

"But Carlo was so fun and welcoming. I can't imagine him being like that."

"As I got older and came out, I noticed things. But when I was younger, I didn't have any context. I just felt sadder and more and more uncomfortable. I wanted to be invisible."

"You weren't. I saw you."

"Could have fooled me. All I wanted was one glance," Paolo said pensively.

"I was afraid of you. I was afraid you would figure out my secret."

"It's too bad. We could have had so much fun."

"We would have gotten into a lot of trouble," Mauro added.

"Speaking of which, you want to go hang out at the pool? I'm finished with my work for the day." All morning Paolo had rehearsed such an overture in his head, and he still wasn't sure what he hoped to accomplish. He feared getting involved, but he had to admit, Mauro looked exceptionally delicious.

Mauro raised a brow and nodded. He had hoped for such an invitation.

"I have a suit you can borrow."

Mauro reached into his shoulder bag and pulled out a red Speedo. "I came prepared."

Paolo's eyes widened. "That's dangerous."

"Intentional."

"Well, well, well." Paolo glanced around. "Are Frank and his team still around?"

"He said they were wrapping up soon."

They both heard a van head down the driveway and onto the roadway. "Speaking of which, sounds like we are alone."

"Why don't you change?"

Mauro retreated while Paolo prepared snacks. He followed Mauro later and went into the main bedroom, where he changed into a pair of trunks and flip-flops. They both met in the hall. Paolo couldn't believe his eyes as he looked down at Mauro's suit. He wasn't sure how long he would be able to maintain self-restraint. "Here's a towel," Paolo said, tossing one to Mauro.

Paolo led them back into the kitchen, where they retrieved food and drinks and headed outside, walking down the hill to the pool and deck. Mauro chose a chaise, rolled out a towel, and sat down, setting his glass of wine on a small side table.

Paolo set his glass down and walked nervously around the deck, adjusting chairs, picking up a few errant leaves, and grabbing the pool net to skim a few blades of grass that were floating on the surface of the water. He kept glancing at Mauro — his skin taking on a sheen as it perspired in the sun, his dark hairy muscular legs extending out from his lean body, and the tantalizing red Speedo doing very little to conceal Mauro's enviable package.

"Come sit down. You're making me nervous," Mauro said.

Paolo set the pool net down and walked toward Mauro, sitting on the adjacent reclining chair.

"Here," Mauro insisted, patting the space next to him.

Paolo rose obediently and sat next to Mauro, pressing his hip against Mauro's thigh. Ill-at-ease and still unsure of what he wanted to happen, Paolo's eyes darted back and forth. He realized that as someone who had been out for some time, he should be taking the initiative. He should be leading and making Mauro more comfortable. But deep down, he felt hesitant and inadequate next to Mauro.

Mauro's drawstring was hanging seductively outside his suit. Nervously, Paolo reached over and tugged on it playfully.

Mauro raised a brow, as if to dare him to continue.

Paolo pulled it closer toward him, and the suit slid down provocatively around Mauro's increasingly firm sex. Despite his reluctance to leap off into the deep end with Mauro, Paolo's breathing accelerated and his heart began to pound as he gazed at the end of Mauro's cock. The soft skin glistened in the sunlight, and Paolo longed to take hold of it. He released the tension on the drawstring, and he ran his hand along the upper band of the suit, grazing the top of Mauro's erection.

He watched Mauro's sex firm up and shift inside the thin fabric. Behind his sunglasses, Mauro seemed unruffled and self-confident, even a bit cocky. Paolo wondered if he dared to stir Adonis. Was he ready for the god's force, for his power, for his regard?

Paolo ran his hand along Mauro's lower abdomen and down toward his sex. Mauro shifted, stirred, moaned. He reached up and took off his glasses. He stared into Paolo's dark eyes as if to say, 'go on.'

Paolo leaned forward and gave Mauro a deep and forceful kiss. Mauro's lips were salty and a bit sweet. He could feel Mauro's hardness pressed against him. He reached behind Mauro and slipped his hands down under the fabric of his suit, and squeezed his round, firm buttocks. They were his now.

Mauro pulled back from their kiss and ran his hand over Paolo's brow. "So playful, irresistible — the same eyes as Carlo's."

Paolo felt self-conscious as he watched Mauro's desire mount. He didn't feel desirable. Then Mauro leaned forward and kissed his nose. He added, "Your nose is so hot. Bold and luscious. I've always wanted to eat it up!"

Paolo shook his head, blushing. He needed to shift the focus of attention. He glanced down and noticed Mauro's sex had fully breached the confines of his suit. Paolo took hold of it — erect, dark, hot. Mauro looked about nervously, and Paolo said, "No one is here. No one can see us."

Mauro leaned back and closed his eyes as Paolo gripped him, stroked him. Paolo realized it would be easy to bring Mauro to a climax, but he wanted to prolong and extend the adventure unfolding between them. He let go of Mauro and ran his hand up and down Mauro's thigh, giving a firm squeeze of his muscles.

"*Non ci posso credere* – still can't believe this," Paolo whispered.

Mauro nodded. "I always wanted you to talk to me in Italian, to come onto me in my own language."

Paolo held his finger up to his lips and said, "Shh." He took the wet finger and pressed it between Mauro's legs. Mauro groaned and closed his eyes. "*Madonna!*" he exclaimed and then he added,

"*Vieni*, come here." He reached for Paolo's trunks and tugged on them. "*Spogliati* – take them off."

Self-consciously, Paolo nodded no. He leaned forward and rested on Mauro's chest, hoping to distract Mauro from his quest. He didn't want him to notice how out of shape he had become. But Mauro slipped his hands inside the folds of the suit and massaged Paolo's buttocks. Adroitly, he slipped the shorts down and reached under, feeling Paolo's erection. "*Ma dai*, come on, I've seen you before."

"I was in better shape then."

"You're incredibly handsome. He ran his hand over Paolo's dark, wavy hair and nudged him to the side. Paolo fell onto his back.

Mauro took a deep breath as he gazed at Paolo's gleaming erect cock. He wasn't exactly sure how things were supposed to work, but he knew he both coveted and feared Paolo's huge shaft. He ran his hand over it, and Paolo trembled.

In his head, Mauro began to formulate questions troubling him. He was in unchartered territory. He wasn't sure what the next move should be.

Paolo sensed Mauro's hesitation, his inexperience. He would have to take control. He fought his own reluctance, a residual fear of letting go, of becoming involved, of – God forbid – falling in love. He wanted to enter Mauro, take possession of his body. He climbed back on top of Mauro and straddled him, resting his cock on Mauro's abdomen.

"You're so fucking sexy," Mauro said in response to the marvel in front of him. He wanted Paolo to enter him. Instinctively, he spat in his hand and reached up, stroking Paolo. Paolo sighed in delight as he felt the warm wetness envelop him, and he slowly guided himself inside Mauro.

Mauro winced and then relaxed, savoring the warmth invading his body. He felt the potency of Paolo's body revive his own, filling the empty spaces that had formed over the years. Being taken by the man inside him felt so natural and right, as if his body and heart had finally found resonance. He felt his skin tighten, his muscles firm up, and his pulse race. He was young again.

Paolo grasped Mauro's cock — firm, thick, and warm. He slid his hand up and down it, observing Mauro close his eyes and slip into an altered state of reality as they both rode waves of pleasure coursing through their bodies. Their breathing increased, their muscles firmed, and their skin became hot.

"Oh my God," Paolo moaned as he plunged himself deeper and deeper into Mauro. With each thrust, he felt the bindings around his heart unravel. "Hmm, hmm," he groaned as he flexed himself, feeling the cords loosen, untie, and spring free. As waves of intense pleasure rode up his body, Paolo fought competing urges — one to hold them back, to save his heart from exploding into a thousand pieces — and the other to let go, to finally to give in to another, fully, completely, unreservedly.

Abandoning all reserve, Paolo let himself go and came in an explosive climax, his cock throbbing inside Mauro. Mauro arched his back and felt his body shudder in Paolo's hands, exploding in spasms of intense pleasure. They both collapsed in each other's arms, panting heavily as they breathed in the scent of their bodies perspiring in the bright sun.

"Oh my god," Mauro murmured as Paolo extracted himself and reclined against his side. Paolo placed his hand affectionately on Mauro's chest and savored the peace that descended on them both.

Mauro eventually stirred. Paolo asked, "Are you okay?"

"Hmm, yes, quite," Mauro replied with a smile.

Paolo raised his brow. "I've created a monster."

"*Andiamo in aqua?*" Mauro asked as he stood and walked toward the pool. He dove in, and Paolo followed.

Paolo swam up to Mauro and grinned. "I'm still not believing the affable Paolo Minetti," Mauro observed.

"And I, the new member of the gay squadron," Paolo remarked as he took hold of Mauro's hand under the water. "You put on quite a performance for a novice."

"Now what?" Mauro asked as they treaded water next to each other.

Paolo wasn't sure what was next. He shook his head pensively. In all his wildest dreams, he would never have imagined such a situation. He watched as Mauro swam to the other side, the whiteness of his buttocks shimmering under the surface of the water. He stopped and turned around, and Paolo gasped for breath. Mauro was strikingly handsome — his caramel skin, his dark hair, his expressive eyes made his heart pound deeply.

Mauro glided past Paolo and pulled himself out of the pool. He reached for his towel and began to dry himself. Paolo joined him and wrapped a towel around his waist. He leaned forward and gave Mauro another kiss. "*Che facciamo adesso?* – What do you want to do now?"

"Have you ever been to Castel Gandolfo?"

"Where's that?"

"Nearby. A small town on Lake Albano — the place where the Popes summered."

"Never been."

"Let's go. We could have a drink there with marvelous views of the lake. Watch the sun go down."

"Okay. Let's get you looking more respectable," Paolo said, glancing up and down Mauro's torso. He grabbed his hand and led him up the hill to the house.

They changed and got into Mauro's car and headed out onto the roadway. The road twisted and turned through the beautiful countryside. Paolo leaned his head back on the seat and gazed out of the window as vineyards, forests, and impressive villas passed by. "It is beautiful here," Paolo admitted.

"Never thought I would hear you say that."

Paolo sighed. "Sometimes it takes a while to appreciate something."

They arrived at a bluff, and the immense volcanic lake of Albano appeared. "Wow!" Paolo remarked as he pressed his face up against the car window. Historic villas lined the crest with amazing views of the lake below.

"That's the village over there," Mauro said, pointing to a medieval town perched on a ridge. "And that's the papal palace," he added, pointing to an imposing structure.

They continued the drive, parked in a small lot, and walked to a café overlooking the water. A handsome waiter came to their table, took their order, and retreated to the inside bar. He returned with their drinks.

"*Salute!*" they both said to each other.

"This is amazing. I wonder if I came here once with Carlo and Luisa. I must have been young. I don't recall it."

"I'm sure they had a lot to do at the vineyard, and they were only here for short periods of time, right?"

"If I recall, they usually came for a visit in the spring to get things ready for the season. They returned to Boston but then came back in August and September for vacation and the harvest."

"Your grandfather must have done well to be able to make trips like that."

Paolo nodded. "He had a successful plumbing business. As he got older, he had associates who could cover for him when he came to Italy."

"Why didn't he just move here? He seemed to like it so much."

"I keep asking myself the same question."

"What do you think about Signor Cipro's offer?"

Paolo looked off pensively. The angle of the light was changing rapidly, turning the sky a beautiful rose color. The shadows of the buildings lengthened, and a refreshing breeze gently caressed the terrace of the café. "It's a reasonable offer, but I'm concerned about all the money I've already spent. When am I going to get it back? Will I ever get it back?"

"So, you still intend on selling it?"

Paolo gave Mauro a curious look. "Of course. Why wouldn't I?"

Mauro felt a pinch in his chest. He hoped that perhaps Paolo might be having second thoughts as the two of them reconnected, that he might at least pause his plans to see what unfolded. "I don't know. Now that you moved into the house, I wondered if you were reconsidering."

"It's just temporary. Why stay in a hotel when I have my own place. Besides, the staging of it will be good for resale."

Mauro nodded pensively and took a large sip of his drink. "So, will you buy Cipro's barn and cellar?"

"I guess I might have to. Carlo's cellar will be off limits. If I want to sell the place as a working vineyard, I need wine equipment and storage space."

"Have you thought about making your own wine?" Mauro inquired.

"Edoardo mentioned that one of the archaeology students knows winemaking. They trimmed the vines in June. If I had a cellar, I guess she could make one more vintage."

"That would be cool. One final salute to Carlo."

Paolo shook his head. He felt betrayed by his grandfather. He finished his drink all at once and set the glass down on the table with force. "I'm not sure I want to salute him or celebrate him. I know that sounds cold and harsh, but given what I know, I don't have a lot of warm feelings about him or the vineyard."

"Sorry," Mauro apologized.

"Not to worry. Everyone liked him. He was a generous and gracious person. He just didn't like having a gay grandson."

Mauro could see the pain in Paolo's face and the tension in his body. Carlo's presence was like a demon, haunting him still. "Should we go?" Mauro suggested.

Paolo nodded and rose, handing the waiter some money. They walked back to the car and drove back to the vineyard.

"Sorry," Paolo said inside the car, placing his hand affectionately on Mauro's leg. "I wish I could be more positive and enthusiastic about the villa, the vineyard, Italy. It's beautiful, and it's been nice to spend time with you."

"I understand," Mauro said thoughtfully. He wished he could get inside Paolo's head and change his memories, take out the bad ones and fill them with happy ones. He hoped their growing connection might have an impact, but as he glanced over at his companion, he wondered if he was irretrievably scarred.

Mauro drove up to the house and got out of the car. He approached Paolo and gave him a warm embrace and said, "Let's get together again soon. I enjoyed it."

Paolo replied, "Me too." He gave Mauro a kiss. "Safe travels home."

Mauro smiled. He had hoped Paolo would have pressed him to stay. The souvenirs of their afternoon by the pool lingered. He wanted more. Perhaps Paolo didn't. He nodded regretfully and got back into his car, driving off toward Rome.

15

Chapter Fifteen – Carlo

The next day, on his way to pick up supplies in Frascati, Paolo passed by the local café, where he noticed Joanna was sipping coffee. He walked briskly past, hoping she wouldn't notice him. Suddenly, he heard, "Paolo, Paolo."

He turned reluctantly, and Joanna stood waving at him.

"Joanna. What a surprise. I didn't see you."

"Join me for a drink."

"I can't. I'm in a bit of a hurry. I have an appointment."

"With whom?"

"Angelo," Paolo said.

"Oh, I just saw him. He was heading off to a property."

"Hmm," Paolo said, caught in his own lie. "Maybe he forgot we were supposed to get together."

"Then have a drink."

Paolo glanced about as if looking for a new pretext to avoid a protracted visit with Joanna and realized he had none. Reluctantly, he nodded and joined her.

"Were you away? I haven't seen you around?"

"I had to go back to Boston to deal with some medical emergencies with my parents." He said, distracted by Joanna's long, tan legs crossed in front of her and the glittery gold sandals she wore.

"Oh, I'm sorry to hear. Are they okay?"

"Not really, but they are being taken care of." Paolo's eyes darted back and forth restlessly.

"And the house?"

"Lots of complications, but it's coming along."

She gave him a look, hoping he would elaborate.

"They found some Roman artifacts. We had to put things on hold for a while."

"How exciting."

"Not really."

"Can I see them?"

"In due time. The archaeologists are doing their thing."

"Well, I have some news."

Paolo quickly waved down the waiter. He was going to need a lot of wine to get through one of Joanna's stories.

The server took his order and returned quickly with a cold glass of local white. Paolo took a long sip and asked, "So, what's the news?"

"I had an interesting chat with my grandmother after you and I visited earlier in the summer. She's getting up there in years, but still has a good memory. I was intrigued by the falling out she and your grandparents had, and I wanted to find out more."

"And?"

"You may already know the story — about Carlo during the war?"

Paolo shook his head no.

"No one ever made reference to his past?"

"No. And Carlo never spoke about that time in his life."

"Well, it's quite a shocking tale." Joanna raised her brows. She continued, "Apparently, Carlo's father, a soldier, died in the war. He and his mother fell on difficult times. Carlo was an exceedingly handsome teenager, and he discovered he could pick up money selling himself – you know – for sex – with men. It helped get them through the tough times."

"No!" Paolo said in disbelief. Blood rushed to his face, and he took another long sip of the wine. "I never knew that about him." Paolo could feel his pulse race as he contemplated the revelations about his grandfather. He tried to imagine him as a teenager walking the streets, cruising potential clients, and engaging in various acts. He shook his head. He let the information sit with him for a while, as he remained speechless.

Joanna worried as she watched Paolo become increasingly quiet, somber. He finally said quietly, ponderously, "So, what does that have to do with the falling out between our grandparents?"

"My grandmother feels terrible." Joanna fidgeted in her chair and fanned herself with the plastic menu. She continued, "Apparently, she made a few comments about him to neighbors. She was jealous of his success in America, the nice vineyard he had in Italy, and the popular parties he threw here. Some friends mentioned how nice he and Luisa were, and she had had enough. She told her friends that he was lucky Luisa would marry him, given his reputation. They, of course, asked what that was, and she described his sordid past."

"That's horrible."

"I know. And she's very apologetic about what she did." Joanna fanned herself nervously.

"She must have tried to make amends."

"She did, but Carlo and Luisa were unforgiving."

"Did she say anything else?"

"Apparently, the reason Carlo and Luisa emigrated to the United States was because he couldn't find work after the war. Too many people knew of his reputation and wouldn't hire him."

Paolo glanced off into the distance, deep in thought. "Perhaps that's why he had such an exaggerated affection for Italy."

"One would have thought just the opposite — that he would have spit on the Italian soil and walked away forever."

"You don't know Carlo. He was quite obstinate. I can fully imagine him saying no one is going to tell me I'm not good enough. I'll show them. And that's what he did. He went to the United States, started a successful business, and came back to Italy to let everyone know he was as Italian as they were. He had a beautiful piece of property, a flourishing vineyard, and a house full of guests all summer long."

"That made my grandmother livid and jealous, particularly after she got uninvited."

"How unfortunate."

"I hope you're not upset."

Paolo fidgeted with the paper napkin resting under his wineglass. He paused and then said, "No. Quite the contrary. It explains a lot. I never understood the passion he had for Italy, for the villa, for his heritage. I resented it. I was an American, and he kept trying to make me into an Italian, into a local, like him. I did everything I could to resist." What Paolo didn't share with Joanna was the connection he now recognized between Carlo's gay slurs and his past.

Joanna nodded, realizing why Paolo was always so *antipatico*. She felt compassion for him, for the subterranean narrative that he was ignorant of and that had played such a role in his life.

"So, our grandparents never reconciled?"

"Apparently not."

"Too bad," Paolo said, his head nodding back and forth in disbelief.

Joanna sat still for a moment and took a sip of her drink. A less contentious subject seemed in order, so she asked, "How did you get archaeologists to work on the property so quickly? Those things usually take ages."

"Remember Mauro?"

Joanna glanced away, searching in her mind for traces of a Mauro. "You mean the guy who came to the farm when we were younger?"

"The very one."

"Well, he's an archaeologist, and he pulled some strings."

"How fortunate."

"Hmm. Yes."

"Does he live around here?"

"In Rome, with his wife – although she just passed."

Pensively, Joanna glanced off into the distance and took a long sip of wine. "Mauro. Hmm. Sorry to hear about that."

"Yes, it was quite sudden. He's struggling to deal with it."

"What's he like?"

"He's an archaeologist. A bit nerdy."

"And he was married?" she asked, raising a brow.

"Yes. He met someone on a dig in Turkey. They have a daughter."

"Did you all visit? What's he been up to? What does he look like?"

"We visited briefly. He seems busy with work. He looks good — looks the same as he did when we were younger." Paolo didn't elaborate on their budding interaction.

"He was so handsome when we were younger. We all were — handsome, beautiful, sexy."

"You still are," Paolo said, giving Joanna a glance. He didn't find her sexy, but he figured it was an appropriate concession to her comment.

"In the right lighting!" she said, chuckling.

Joanna took a sip of her drink, and Paolo finished his glass in one final gulp. The references to Mauro and the story about his grandfather hit him all of a sudden. He felt his chest tighten and his legs become weak and wobbly. He feared his body would take on a mind of its own, and he would lose control of himself. He grasped the edge of the table, stood, and tossed some coins onto the table. "Sorry. I have to go."

Joanna stood and looked imploringly into his eyes. "I hope I didn't upset you."

Paolo nodded no and walked away.

He turned a corner and leaned against the wall of a building. His legs felt like they would give way under him, and he felt dizzy, lightheaded. "Oh, shit. I'm going to pass out," he mumbled in alarm. He sat on the pavement with his head down, hoping it would pass.

A few moments later, an elderly woman placed her hands on his shoulder and asked if he was okay. "*Lei sta bene?*"

He glanced up at her caring face and nodded yes. "*Si, grazie. Sto bene.*" He slowly stood and leaned against the wall for a moment, regaining strength. She peered at him, and he repeated that he was fine. But he wasn't. She walked away. He glanced at his surroundings and struggled to remember where he was and where he had parked his car. "What the fuck?" he murmured to himself.

Slowly, he found his way to the parking lot, found his automobile, and headed back to the farm. He pulled up to the house and walked inside, plopping himself down on the sofa in the living room.

He began to shake, and tears flowed down his cheeks. Everything now made sense, but it didn't make things right. He was angry and felt deceived. Not only had his grandfather shamed him, but he had his own secrets, his own indiscretions. He should have been more understanding, but instead, had been relentless in trying to exorcise any gay tendencies in his grandson.

He fought competing emotions — compassion for all his grandparents went through and overcame — and resentment at being played, manipulated, shamed. He realized he must have disappointed them, rubbing salt in wounds that ran deep. It was amazing how they overcame adversity and built a thriving business in Boston and a lovely vineyard in Italy.

Yet he had been an impressionable teen, and they belittled and undermined his emerging sexuality — his nascent desires, fantasies, and longings. No wonder he had been unable to sustain any relationship. Each developing romance fell victim to self-sabotaging doubts, fears, disgrace.

He glanced around the room with great ambivalence. The house represented Carlo's attempt to say *'vaffanculo – fuck you'* to the mean-spirited people who turned their backs on him. He could appreciate the bravado of it all. Yet the same righteousness ended up poisoning him. Paolo tried to add his own touch and aesthetics to the place, and he liked how it had turned out. There was a part of him that was intrigued by the idea of owning a vineyard, becoming a vintner, and traveling back and forth to Italy. But he wasn't sure he could ever make peace with the place where his dreams and desires had been reviled and undermined.

16

Chapter Sixteen – The Holy Family

Paolo spent considerable time brooding over the information he had learned about his grandfather. He needed to talk with someone, get things off his chest, and make sense of things. A day later, he called Mauro.

"Mauro, how are you?"

"Good. I enjoyed the other day."

The image of their intimate afternoon flashed before Paolo's eyes. He blushed and said, "Hmm. Me, too. What are you up to today?"

"Nothing much. Why?"

"Remember the painting in the house, the Holy Family, in the dining room?"

"Yes."

"I'd like to see the original. It's by Andrea del Sarto, and I believe it is in the Palazzo Barberini."

"Yes. I know it. It's there."

"If I come into town, could you meet me at the museum?"

"Sure. What did you have in mind?"

"Say three or four this afternoon?"

"There's a fountain in Piazza Barberini. I can meet you there at four o'clock."

"*A presto.*"

Later that afternoon, Paolo approached Bernini's famous Fountain of the Triton, where water was splashing in the afternoon sunlight and noisy traffic circled the square. He noticed Mauro leaning languorously against a light post, checking messages on his phone. His face sparkled in the light, and his dark hair danced in the breeze. As he looked up and noticed Paolo, there was an intense allure in his eyes. "*Ciao,*" Paolo said as he approached.

Mauro gave him a warm embrace and said, "It's good to see you."

"Yes, thanks for coming. *Andiamo?*" he suggested.

They walked up the hill and approached a beautiful palace. They went inside, bought tickets, and climbed a beautiful staircase to the main gallery area. Mauro poked his head into a few rooms until he found the painting.

"Here it is."

"Yes. This is the one. Wow!"

"It's impressive."

"It meant so much to Carlo," Paolo began.

"It's rather well known in art circles, noteworthy for its unique style, color, and composition."

Paolo stood quietly, contemplating the piece. His eyes became red and watery. Mauro looked over and noticed.

"*Che c'e?* What's up?"

"I always felt a certain disdain for this. It felt like Carlo's way of waving the idea of the perfect family in my face, pressuring me to marry an Italian girl and have Italian babies."

"And now?"

"I've come to learn some things that shed new light on it."

Mauro returned a curious look.

"We can talk about it later."

"Preview?"

"Look at Mary and Jesus. They are both glancing at something, something that causes apprehension or consternation. Jesus is pulling in his shoulders to protect himself. It's as if he has a secret, and Mary seems to have some inkling of it."

Mauro shook his head. He gazed at the painting. It seemed to him to be the typical depiction of the Holy Family — Joseph looking protectively on while Mary and Jesus, the focus of attention, embrace each other. "What do you think that is?"

"Well, it could be Jesus' own identity. It's unknown to others, yet he is aware of it. Perhaps Mary is aware, too, or at least suspects." Paolo thought of Carlo's secret, one his mother must have known.

"And Joseph?" Mauro inquired.

"That's a good question. He's in the background, seemingly unimportant, almost absent. Yet he is also looking over them protectively." He wondered if for Carlo, the figure of Joseph was Carlo himself or perhaps his deceased father looking over them from another world.

Paolo continued to study the painting, and tears formed in his eyes. It no longer represented the ideal family. The Holy Family had secrets, and the relationships between them weren't as they appeared.

Mauro reached his arm around Paolo's shoulder and gave him a warm embrace. Paolo wiped his eyes. He turned and walked away, and Mauro followed.

They walked outside into the bright light. Paolo took out a handkerchief and dried his face. Mauro was at a loss for words.

"Do you want to come to my place? We could have something to drink, and you could tell me more."

Paolo nodded, and they made the short trek to Mauro's condo. Once inside, Mauro poured them drinks, and they sat on the sofa.

"So, what's up?"

"I don't know where to begin," Paolo said. "Remember Joanna?"

"Vaguely. She's one of your cousins, right?"

Paolo nodded.

"Her grandmother and my grandmother are sisters. There was a falling out between them."

"Over what?"

"This is where it gets very interesting. I'm not sure I will be able to get it all out without getting emotional." Paolo took a couple of deep breaths.

"Joanna's grandmother was jealous of Carlo and Luisa, and she spread some vicious gossip about them."

"That being?"

Paolo hesitated. He then said, "Apparently, during the Second World War, Carlo's father died as a soldier. He and his mother struggled financially in his absence. Carlo was a teenager, a very handsome and playful one. He discovered that he could make a lot of money turning tricks."

Mauro shook his head as if he didn't understand.

"He had sex with men for money."

"Oh!" Mauro exclaimed. "Shit!"

"Yes. Shit."

"So, what happened?"

"Apparently after the war, he found it difficult to get work. His reputation was damaged; people were afraid to trust him, bring them into their businesses. That's when he and Luisa decided to go to America and start their own enterprise. He was successful and returned each year to take care of his mother and to tend the land that he inherited from his grandfather."

"Wow! I would never have guessed. And Carlo never talked about his father, about the war, about why he left Italy?"

"No. That's what's interesting. He seemed to love everything Italian but avoided talking about earlier times."

"Maybe since he was forced to leave, his affections for his homeland were exaggerated," Mauro hypothesized.

"I'm beginning to suspect that is the case."

"So, what is the connection with the Holy Family?"

"I think it was Carlo's way of compensating for what he sensed were the imperfections and secrets of his own family. He held up the Holy Family proudly. But somehow, he was drawn to Andrea del Sarto's composition — the brooding Joseph and the uneasy looks of Jesus and Mary."

"So, do you think Carlo was gay?" Mauro inquired, rubbing his chin pensively.

"No. I don't think so. He and Luisa were very passionate, and he always seemed to have a thing for the pretty girls gathered at the pool."

"But how is that possible? How could he have had sex with so many men and not have felt some kind of attraction or pleasure?" Mauro pressed.

"Maybe it was purely transactional."

"But surely there had to be something. You can't go through the motions and not feel arousal and enjoyment."

"We are all guilty of doing things without feeling, without sentiment. It's how we protect ourselves."

"That's so cynical."

"I don't mean we do it all the time."

Mauro paused and considered his and Anna's relationship and realized Paolo might have a point.

"So, do you think Carlo knew? About us?"

"What was there to know?"

"Our inclinations."

"I don't think he suspected you were so inclined. He always wanted me to be like you. But he was dead set on keeping me in line, shaming me into being straight. It's so hypocritical. I'm so angry," Paolo said, leaning forward on the sofa and turning red in the face.

"You have to let that go. Forgive him. It was a different time."

"It wasn't that long ago."

"Think about it, though. When he was a teenager, he was exploited."

"He made money. He was soliciting clients," Paolo noted.

"He was poor, and rich older men took advantage of him. He saw homosexuality as exploitative, promiscuous, and devoid of love."

Paolo realized Mauro might be right, but he retorted, "But years later, things were different. He should have grown with the times."

"Maybe he couldn't see the difference. He saw what he had experienced, and he didn't want you to be taken advantage of."

"He stole my adolescence. He stole my adulthood. He stole any chance for me to find love."

"Last time I checked, while you might not be a sexy teenager, you are one hot man who someone finds lovable."

"I'm damaged goods."

"We all are. That's what relationships are about. They are where we become vulnerable and realize we are lovable."

Paolo shook his head.

Mauro ran his hand over Paolo's back. He was warm and feverish. "Forgive him. He loved you and wanted to protect you."

"He was hateful, narrow-minded, and stubborn."

"He's gone. You are now the author of your life."

"I'm tired."

"It takes a lot of energy to keep everything in and try to be what others want. Believe me, I know."

"I just can't pivot."

"You don't have to achieve it all at once. Take little steps," Mauro said thoughtfully.

"I should be encouraging you. You've lost your wife, and you are coming out. That's huge."

"No more daunting than unraveling years of internalized shame."

"I don't know if I can do it."

"That's because you believed Carlo; you were convinced your dreams were flawed. But he was mistaken. Accept that you are handsome, talented, resourceful, and capable of wonderful love, and you will discover the energy."

"I'm still not convinced."

"Let's start small. I think you're terribly sexy. I'd love to take you to dinner. One step at a time."

"But," Paolo began.

Mauro put his finger on Paolo's lips. "Shh. Sexy man, come have dinner with me." Mauro grabbed Paolo's hand and led him outside onto the street.

17

Chapter Seventeen – Vintner

Paolo heard his phone vibrate nearby. Disoriented in a dark, unfamiliar room, he stretched out his arm. His hand grazed Mauro's chest. He stirred. "*Buongiorno, tesoro.* Hello, dear."

"My phone."

"*Ecco,*" Mauro mumbled, retrieving it and handing it to Paolo.

"*Pronto,*" Paolo answered.

"Paul, this is Angelo. How are you doing? Where are you? I'm at the vineyard."

"I'm running errands."

Angelo looked around and said, "But your car is here."

"In Rome."

"How did you get to the station?"

"Frank dropped me."

Angelo noticed Frank wasn't around. He raised a brow.

"Shit," Paolo whispered to himself, realizing his story was flimsy. Frank was taking the day off.

"Well, anyway, I am calling because Signor Cipro needs a decision on the barn and cellar. Someone wants to buy his equipment, but he doesn't want to get rid of it if you aren't going to move forward."

"Hmm, I'm conflicted. I just don't have the money, and I don't think the sale will fetch enough to justify more expenses."

"I have been thinking about that. What if you listed the vineyard without a cellar but with the option of buying an adjoining one? No one is going to want to buy the vineyard without a cellar, so they will opt in, and you will get extra money, money you can quantify as additional."

"You're very clever, Angelo."

"I know this is stressful, and I want you to realize a good return."

"When would Cipro need money?"

"That's where there's even better news. As long as you sign papers promising the purchase, he will accept funds anytime in the next twelve months. So, you aren't out any money in advance."

"Wow. I can't think of any reason not to move forward, then."

"I thought that would be your answer. Cipro will sell his equipment. I reached out to Edoardo, who said he can move Carlo's fermentation vats into Cipro's building before the harvest — that is, if you would like to produce wine."

"Sophia, one of Frank's students, grew up on a vineyard. She said she is willing to supervise. But I don't know. It's a lot of work, trouble, and cost." What Paolo didn't convey to Angelo was his new resentment of Carlo and eagerness to find closure and move on.

"Spend money. Make money."

"Did Edoardo coach you?"

"A good vintage will increase the value of the estate significantly."

"What if it is not a good vintage?"

"We won't tell anyone if it's not good. The property would still be valuable without a recent production."

Paolo glanced towards the other side of the bed. Mauro was stirring. His morning erection was impressive, and he wanted to get rid of Angelo so he could take care of other things, more appetizing things.

"Okay. *Va bene.* Draw papers, let Cipro know, and line Edoardo up to move equipment. Gotta go. *Ciao.*"

Angelo looked at his phone and shook his head at the hasty conclusion of his talk with Paolo. He got into his car and returned to his office.

Paolo crawled toward Mauro and licked the side of his pecs. "Hey delicious thing!"

Mauro pretended to be groggy, half asleep, but he ran his hand down over his cock and began to play with it.

"Now you're just teasing me," Paolo said, lifting himself up on top of Mauro and staring into his dark brown eyes.

"I was playing with myself, but if you want to join, I'm happy to accommodate."

Paolo's own sex began to firm up, and he rubbed it over Mauro's taut abdomen. Mauro groaned as he felt its solidity and heat.

"Your turn."

Mauro gave Paolo a quizzical look. Paolo rolled off of Mauro and reclined next to him, his firm, round buttocks ripe for the taking. Mauro's eyes opened wide in amazement.

He ran his hands over Paolo, who quivered in anticipation. Mauro felt his pulse quicken and the edge of his sex throb. He pulled himself on top of Paolo and reached his arms around his chest. Nuzzling his sex in the folds of Paolo's body, he breathed in Paolo's scent and affectionately kissed his back.

Paolo savored the weight of Mauro on top of him, the security and affection he felt in his arms, and the promise of Mauro consuming him.

Mauro nudged himself into the folds of Paolo's buttocks. Their skin was moist from perspiration, and he pressed himself in without much effort. "*Madonna!*" he exclaimed as he slowly but firmly moved back and forth, feeling the tightness of Paolo around him. "I want to see you," he interjected, taking hold of Paolo's shoulder and turning him over. Mauro easily re-entered Paolo, staring into his beguiling eyes. Paolo's indifference had turned to a childlike contentment — a playful energy that Mauro found irresistible, given their past antagonism. He watched Paolo close his eyes and savor Mauro's force and power.

Paolo clutched Mauro and pulled him close. He longed to close the spaces that had formed between them when they were younger. He yearned to knit together the fragments of his own life, to feel his body and fantasies become one.

"*Quanto sei bello, quanto sei sexy* – how handsome, how sexy," Mauro murmured to Paolo as he leaned back up and ran his hands over Paolo's abdomen and took hold of him. With Paolo in his hands, he felt their flesh become one, the sensations of each reinforcing the other — a crescendo of warmth, vibration, and tremors of intense pleasure coursing up and down their bodies. Mauro continued to thrust himself deeper and deeper into Paolo, gazing into his eyes. Soon, he felt ripples race through his body into an explosive climax – his body thrashing inside of and on top of Paolo. He felt contractions in the flesh he held, and watched as Paolo came, too. Mauro collapsed onto Paolo, resting his head on his chest, and breathed in his distinctive scent. Neither was eager to move. Paolo relished the firmness of Mauro's body on top of him; he felt safe, embraced, and grounded.

Mauro finally rose and went to the bathroom, returning with a towel. Paolo grinned as Mauro cleaned him and gazed into his eyes.

"Breakfast?" Mauro asked, breaking the reverent silence between them.

"Coffee."

"*Subito*, right away."

Paolo went into the bathroom, washed up, and put on his clothes. He wandered into the kitchen where Mauro, in nothing more than his underwear, was preparing two double espressos. He handed one to Paolo, who breathed in the aroma and took a long sip.

"Was that Angelo on the phone?" Mauro inquired.

Paolo nodded groggily.

"What did he want?"

"A decision on Cipro's cellar."

"What did you decide?"

"I told him to move forward. But I'm still conflicted."

Mauro wasn't conflicted, and Paolo's words made him uneasy.

"Why?"

"I just can't afford any more expenses, and I'm angry at Carlo — not sure I want to embrace his world, his dreams."

"You don't have to. You can make them your own."

"But everywhere I look, I see him; I see Luisa."

"I see you," Mauro said warmly.

"I see you, too," Paolo said without a lot of emotion or enthusiasm.

Mauro wondered if he simply felt compelled to repay the sentiment. "Will you make wine?"

"I guess so. At least one last vintage."

"After all these years, we have a vintner in our midst," Mauro said enthusiastically, masking his increased apprehension.

"I'm not sure I would use that term. Sophia is the one who will be responsible for the whole process."

"What's the timeframe?"

"I don't know. I'll have to ask her when she thinks the grapes will be ready and how we are going to find sufficient people to help."

"That shouldn't be difficult. Between her classmates and Edoardo's crew, you already have a good start. I'm sure they can all recruit a few more as well."

The thought of the harvest and all the work that needed to be done to prepare for it startled Paolo. He suddenly became restless, and beads of sweat formed on his brow. "I have to go. I need to speak with Sophia and Edoardo."

"I thought we were going to go sightseeing."

"Sorry. With these new developments, I realize I have a lot of work to do. Rain check?"

Mauro nodded. He gave Paolo an enthusiastic kiss, turned him around, and said, "Go, Signor Minetti. Make your wine!"

Paolo pivoted and smiled. He leaned forward and gave Mauro a final kiss. "I'll be in touch."

"Ciao."

Paolo walked out of the door and headed to the station, where he caught a train back to Frascati and took a taxi to the vineyard.

18

Chapter Eighteen – The Vendemmia

A week later, everything was set for the harvest. Edoardo and his crew had moved fermentation vats, oak barrels, wine racks, and other equipment into Signor Cipro's cellar. Sophia astutely supervised the placement of things and recruited nearly twenty people to help gather the grapes. The day of the *vendemmia* was still to be determined, contingent on the weather and the condition of the ripening fruit.

A few days later, Paolo walked with Sophia in the field. "So, what do you think?"

Sophia strolled slowly between rows of vines. She breathed in the early autumn air. She sensed that Mother Nature was ready to give birth, to yield her bounty. She took a bunch of grapes in her hand and said, "They have just the right give and take — the skin is perfect. The weather for the next couple of days should be clear and not too warm." She inserted a device into the fruit to measure the sugar content. "Hmm, this should be a good harvest, and we will make an excellent wine."

Paolo felt his heart race with excitement. "How do you know?"

"Past vintages have been good, and I'm impressed with how Carlo's wine holds up over time. We don't have these varietals in New York, but they are perfect for this region. The sugar content is ideal. Could we harvest the day after tomorrow?"

"It's your call. I think everyone is ready."

"Let's let everyone know. We can get started at seven o'clock. I think with twenty people and an early start, we can finish by two in the afternoon. If you can arrange a nice luncheon, everyone will be happy."

Two days later, cars, vans, and trucks arrived at the vineyard. The sky was crystal clear, and the air was dry and pleasant. Paolo had ordered coffee and croissants to greet everyone on their arrival.

Sophia's classmates drove up first, thrilled with the novelty of a wine harvest in Italy. They wore long-sleeved cotton shirts, jeans, and work boots — their typical archaeological attire. Several had recruited friends who were studying in Rome. Excitedly, they pounced on the coffee and croissants and began to chat enthusiastically about the day ahead of them.

Edoardo drove up in his van, and four men got out of the back, ready to work. Gino followed him up the driveway in his own truck. He brought three friends. Paolo gasped for air as Gino exited the driver's seat. He hadn't seen him since earlier in the summer, and he'd forgotten how cute he was. He had an uncanny resemblance to Mauro and seemed aware of his impact on Paolo, smiling warmly at him as he led his friends forward.

"Paolo, these are my friends — Luigi, Bruno, and Alex. *Questo è Paolo*," Gino concluded, raising a brow playfully. Gino's friends gazed at Paolo and nodded, whispering to one another. Gino had already shared his fascination with the moody American, and they knew he still hoped to seduce him.

Everyone extended their hands warmly. "Thanks for your help," Paolo said, gesturing for them to help themselves to coffee and pastries. Gino accompanied his friends, but his eyes were fixed on Paolo.

Mauro was the last to arrive, having driven in from Rome. He pulled up the driveway and parked behind Gino's truck. He stepped out of his car and nodded to Paolo, who walked up to him and gave him a chaste embrace to maintain appearances.

Soon Paolo yelled, "*Attenzione, prego,*" hoping to gather everyone together for instructions. "This is Sophia. She is in charge. She is a winemaker – *una enologa* – from New York."

The Italians murmured to each other, incredulous that New York made wine or that a woman would be in charge.

Sophia stepped forward and said, "*Buongiorno. Grazie per il vostro aiuto* – thanks for your help. Edoardo and his crew will place baskets at the end of each row. Here are clippers," she added, pointing to Piero, who began to distribute them to each person.

She added, "We hope to finish by two o'clock, and then Paolo will provide a big lunch for us."

Everyone nodded and smiled.

"Each person can take a row. When your basket is full, let Edoardo know, and he will dump it in the trailer. Then go to the next free row and continue. You probably know this already — try to keep leaves out of the baskets, and if a bunch is rotten or surrounded by some kind of infestation, leave it on the vine. There are water bottles available at several small tables in the field. Any questions?"

People shook their heads, eager to get to work.

"*Allora – al lavoro* – to work!"

It had been years since Paolo had harvested grapes. He walked into the field and chose a free row of vines and began clipping the bunches and tossing them into the straw basket near his feet. He kicked it along and continued to clip the grapes. Soon, his forearms were sticky with grape juice, and pesky gnats began to circle nearby. He chuckled as he peered over at some of Sophia's friends, who undoubtedly thought the day would be a romantic romp through an idyllic Italian vineyard. He knew the work was grueling and that one's muscles and back would ache soon.

Strategically, Gino wedged his way into the adjacent row and paced himself in order to shadow Paolo as best he could. As the morning warmed and he began to sweat, Gino removed his shirt and stretched. He winked at Paolo through an open section of the vines. "Hmm," Paolo said to himself. "If he thinks I'm daddy material, he's in for a rude awakening. Although he is cute."

Paolo stood and stretched, looking out over the field. Mauro was a few rows down. Like Sophia's colleagues, he came prepared with cargo shorts, leather work boots, and a long-sleeved white shirt. Periodically, he removed his baseball cap and wiped perspiration from his forehead. His dark hair glistened in the sun.

As Paolo watched from afar, he noticed one of Gino's friends, Alex – perhaps about forty-years-old – had positioned himself in the row next to Mauro's. He had a certain appeal — playful salt and pepper hair, expressive eyes, and an enviable physique. Chatty, he engaged Mauro in conversation as they made their way on opposite sides of the vines. "*Cazzo!*" Paolo said with exasperation as he watched Mauro become progressively friendly with his new admirer.

Paolo retrieved a bottle of water from one of the tables and walked toward them. "Do you guys need any water? Everything going well?"

"Paolo, have you met Alex? He's Gino's friend – from Marino."

"*Piacere*," Paolo said as he extended his hand. He scrutinized him carefully, noting Alex's not-so-hidden roving eyes. Mauro's shirt had become wet with perspiration, and his formidable chest was increasingly visible through the translucent fabric. Alex seemed fixated.

"You have a nice vineyard," Alex said. "You must be proud of it."

"It was my grandfather's. Unfortunately, I have to sell it," Paolo said as he glanced at Mauro.

Mauro avoided Paolo's eyes and returned to clipping grapes.

"That's too bad. I would love to have a place like this."

"What do you do for a living?"

"I'm a physician."

"Ahh," Paolo sighed, realizing Alex would be quite the catch. Alex's remark was not lost on Mauro, who looked up from his work. "And how do you know Gino?"

"Through mutual friends," he said, without elaboration.

"Well, thanks for your help. If you need anything, let me know," Paolo concluded, walking back to the row he had been working.

Everyone made good progress. Edoardo and one of his crew collected the full baskets and dumped them into the trailer hooked to Carlo's tractor. When the trailer was full, he took it to Cipro's cellar, where Sophia readied the crushing machine and the fermentation vats.

The day grew increasingly warm. People worked more slowly as their muscles tired. Paolo walked back and forth between the field and the cellar, checking on Sophia's work. At one o'clock, there were only a few rows left to harvest. Paolo confirmed delivery of food from a local trattoria and supervised the assembly of makeshift tables and cloths for the luncheon he had planned.

At two, everyone had finished work. People rinsed off with a few garden hoses, changed shirts, and gathered at the table. When the food was set out, Paolo stood and got everyone's attention. "Thanks for your work and help today. This is the first *vendemmia* at the Minetti vineyard in ten years. I have several people to thank for making this happen. First of all – Angelo, my broker and lawyer, who encouraged me to set up a new cellar and make wine."

Angelo waved to the crowd, who clapped.

"I want to thank the archaeologist amongst us, Mauro, who, applying the regulations of the government, forced me to delay the sale of the vineyard." Mauro blushed, and everyone chuckled and clapped.

"Most of all, I want to thank Sophia, who came all the way from New York to make an excellent Italian wine! She was part of the team excavating the cellar. It's amazing that her colleagues uncovered the remains of an ancient grotto and cellar where Romans made wine. Two thousand years later, we are carrying on those traditions."

People nodded emotionally, cognizant of being immersed in so much history.

Paolo continued, "In all seriousness, many of you have forced me to pause, to take some time, to reacquaint myself with this land and its people. I want to toast Carlo and Luisa, who made this such a special place." He glanced up at the sky. "You were always throwing parties. Here's one in your honor. *Salute!*"

Everyone yelled, "*Salute.*" They sat down and began to eat with abandon.

Mauro glanced at Paolo and wondered if Paolo's antipathy toward his grandfather was melting. His toast to them was a good sign. His affection for him continued to grow, and he hoped Paolo might decide to remain in Italy.

The local trattoria had prepared platters of grilled vegetables, a mixture of grilled meat – chicken, veal, and beef, and plates of pasta coated in homemade pesto. Paolo had retrieved as many of Carlo's drinkable bottles from the cellar as possible and added bottles of red wine from Tuscany. Everyone enjoyed the food and wine.

At around four, people began to leave. Sophia's colleagues left first, visibly exhausted from the hard work. Edoardo's crew and friends left next. Gino and his friends seemed in no hurry to leave, walking up to Paolo and asking if they might take a swim. Paolo hesitated, increasingly agitated that Alex was so friendly with Mauro. But he couldn't say no, not after all the work they had done in the field. "Yeah, sure, enjoy yourselves," he said, retrieving some towels from the house and opening the deck umbrellas for shade.

Gino slipped quickly into an orange Speedo and grabbed one of the chaises on the deck, plopping himself down in the bright sunshine. Paolo gasped for air as he gazed at Gino's lean, muscular body gleaming in the light. Luigi and Bruno had changed in Gino's truck and settled onto a couple of chairs off to the side. They seemed like they might be a couple. Alex slipped into a black Speedo near the truck and took a chaise adjacent to Gino's.

Paolo searched for Mauro, who was missing. Soon, he spied him exiting the house in his red Speedo, traversing the lawn toward the pool. He sat down next to Alex.

"Well, this is a problem," Paolo said to himself as he felt his blood pressure rise. He went inside the house, changed into his suit, and returned to the pool, reclining on one of the chairs across from Alex and Mauro. He put on his glasses, opened a book, but kept his eyes fixed on the two of them.

Gino rose, sauntered toward Paolo, and sat down on Paolo's chaise. "Thanks for the pool," he said, winking at Paolo.

Paolo blushed and nodded. "Thanks for your help."

"*Un piacere*," Gino responded. "Go in pool? *Insieme*, together?"

"No. I need to rest," Paolo said, wanting to keep his eye on Mauro and Alex.

Gino looked disappointed and leaped into the water. He swam back and forth and then pulled himself out and reclined on his chaise. He adjusted himself. Beads of water formed on his torso and sparkled in the bright light. His formidable package was obvious for everyone to see – even his friend Alex couldn't keep from looking.

Paolo chuckled nervously as he surveyed the deck – a veritable gaggle of Italian gay men enjoying the sun, water, and picturesque setting.

Alex leaned toward Mauro and said something in a subdued voice. Mauro laughed in response, playfully slapping Alex's forearm.

Paolo grew angry. He pretended to read as he observed them attentively.

Luigi and Bruno fell asleep, and Gino continued to adjust himself, peering at Paolo as he did so. "Let it go, young man," Paolo whispered to himself. "I'm not buying – although it might be appetizing."

Mauro jumped into the pool to cool down. Alex dove in after him, gliding along the surface of the water as he watched Mauro swim a couple of laps. When Mauro finished swimming, Alex approached and splashed him. Mauro splashed back, and then Alex dunked him, seizing him from behind. They splashed about playfully. Then Alex let go, and they both got out of the pool, their cocks slightly stiff. Gino and Paolo both noticed, exchanged a glance, and then Paolo got up angrily, returning to the house.

The kitchen was a mess, so he cleaned dishes and organized leftover food. Irritated, he looked for more tasks to occupy himself. He spruced up the living room, picked up loose papers, and filed away some books he had recently read. After half an hour, he heard Gino's truck head down the driveway and out onto the road.

Mauro walked inside. "Paolo, are you around?"

"In here," he replied.

Mauro walked into the living room with nothing on but his red Speedo and flip-flops. He approached Paolo, who had taken a seat on the sofa, and ran his hand over Paolo's shoulder.

"What a beautiful day. You must be happy," Mauro said.

Paolo shook Mauro's hand off his shoulder and said sarcastically, "Very happy."

"It's amazing that you were able to finish the harvest in one day," Mauro added.

"Yeah. There was a lot of help," Paolo said, with little emotion.

"Sophia has already crushed the grapes and has started the process of making wine. I can't wait to see what she does."

"Me neither."

"Do you want some coffee?"

"No."

"Some water?"

"No."

"Some of this?" he asked, gesturing at his crotch.

"I don't do leftovers," he said angrily.

"*Tesoro*, what's wrong?" Mauro asked, realizing Paolo was not in a good mood.

"Alex is what's wrong."

Mauro gave Paolo a questioning glance.

Paolo didn't want to have to spell it out, but he did. "Alex was eating you up. Right in front of me and everyone else."

"He did come on a bit strong."

"Strong's not the word. He was insatiable."

"He was just trying to be friendly."

"And you — were you just being friendly when you were drooling all over him, grabbing each other in the pool?"

"I wasn't drooling."

"You could have fooled me."

"Why are you upset?"

"Oh, I don't know. I thought we had an understanding."

"What kind of understanding?" Mauro inquired.

"That there was something here."

"Of course, there's something here."

"Then why flirt with Alex?"

"I wasn't flirting with him. He was flirting with me. It felt reassuring that even at my age, another man might find me attractive."

"So, us?" Paolo asked emphatically.

Mauro glared at Paolo and hesitated. It was clear he wanted to say something, but was measuring his words carefully. "Okay. What about us?"

"What about it?"

"You keep talking about going back to Boston, selling the vineyard, making a return on your expenses. How do you think that makes me feel?"

The truth of Mauro's words hit Paolo like a ton of bricks. He hadn't considered how his indecisiveness might cause him concern, worry, uncertainty.

"I'm sorry. I can see that would cause doubts."

"And so?"

"And so, what?" Paolo pressed.

"Where is all of this going?"

"I don't know," Paolo began hesitantly. "My parents, my life, and my work are in Boston. I'm angry at Carlo for his hypocrisy and manipulation. And I don't see how I can sustain the place. And Angelo says there is a serious buyer."

"So, are there any buts?"

"Of course, there are. The place has grown on me. I love the renovations. I love the fact that we are making Minetti wine again. The vineyard is beautiful. You've opened my eyes to Italian art and history. My hostility to everything here has melted. I like it here."

Mauro felt his heart skip a beat, and his legs grew weak. Paolo hadn't mentioned him, hadn't made any reference to their growing affection for each other. He thought in his head, '*Ma vaffanculo* – fuck you, you self-absorbed son-of-a-bitch.'

Mauro glanced at his watch. "I need to get back to Rome."

"*Resta* – stay. We can talk."

"No, I have to get going," Mauro said, clearly disappointed at what had transpired.

Paolo reached for Mauro's arm and said, "I'm sorry. Stay. We can work this out."

"It's late. I have to go."

"Do you need some fresh clothes?"

"I have some in my bag. I'll change and head out." Mauro walked to the back of the house, retrieved his clean jeans and tee shirt, put them on, and then returned to the living room. Paolo was deep in thought. He wanted to believe Paolo was self-aware, that he might make connections and say the right thing in the end. He walked up to him and gave him a kiss.

"*Ciao, Mauro.* I'll call you," Paolo said with a furrowed brow.

"*Grazie. Ci vediamo.* See you around."

Mauro got into his car, turned on the ignition, and then dialed Angelo's number.

"*Pronto. Mauro?*"

"Yes, it's me. Angelo, I'm sorry to say, I want to withdraw my offer for Paolo's vineyard."

"You're kidding?"

"I wish I were. After much consideration, I don't think it's a good idea. You'll need to put it back on the market."

"I thought you and Paolo were getting along nicely."

"Me too. But he's still insufferable. It's not a good idea."

"I'm sorry to hear. If you reconsider, let me know."

"I will. *Ciao.*"

"*Ciao.*"

19

Chapter Nineteen – Solitary

Both Mauro and Paolo retreated to their respective worlds, nursing disappointments that had festered for decades. Paolo busied himself with work and checking in on Sophia, who was making Minetti wine. Mauro took care of unresolved matters regarding Anna's estate and slowly returned to his own work.

They exchanged superficially friendly texts but made no plans to get together, both fearful of the growing rift that was forming between them. It was easier to ignore what was happening and distract themselves with tasks.

About a week later, Frank called a meeting. He wanted to update everyone on the progress of the excavation. Everyone gathered in front of the archaeological site – Frank and his crew, Angelo, Paolo, and Mauro. Frank began, "Thank you everyone for coming today to hear our final report. It's been an exciting project. We had hoped to uncover another figure in the rubble under the reconstructed medieval floor, but we have only pieced together one. There are some single tiles in the soil and a few small fragments of a mosaic, but not enough for us to continue with any hope of finding another portrait. This one," he said as he pointed to the nude bather, "is magnificent. But he remains solitary."

Frank's words hit Mauro like a ton of bricks. The allusion to a solitary figure was uncanny, an unintentional punctuation mark to a long, curious, but ultimately disappointing summer. He furtively peered toward Paolo, who seemed absorbed by Frank's presentation of the history of the project and its future.

"The reconstructed bather will be exhibited in the local archaeological museum. This grotto will become a satellite excavation site available for special visits. A permanent perimeter will be built to protect it."

Angelo nodded and smiled at Paolo.

"Thanks for all of your hospitality," Frank continued, looking at Paolo and the others. "And we look forward to some of Carlo's new wine once it is ready," he concluded, smiling at Sophia.

Frank stepped away from the table where he had been making remarks and shook Mauro's hand. He approached Paolo and gave him a warm embrace. "I guess we will see you in Boston at some point."

"That would be nice," Paolo replied.

Angelo walked up to Mauro and asked in a quiet voice, "Are you sure you don't want to move forward with the purchase?"

"Unfortunately, yes. If Paolo showed more enthusiasm for us, I would."

"He's preoccupied with his parents and work."

"I get it. But if there's not something more that accompanies that, a craving or passion to find a way forward, then I'm wasting my time."

Angelo looked off toward Paolo and then back again at Mauro. He had witnessed their reunion, the tension that simmered under the surface, a few sparks of passion, and then their mutual retreat into long-established patterns of antipathy. He liked Mauro. He liked Paolo. And he realized they were destined for each other. They just needed a push, a strong one.

He took Mauro's arm and led him toward Paolo. He pushed Mauro toward Paolo. Facing each other, their eyes glanced off evasively, both hoping to maintain the fragile shells they had erected around their hearts.

Angelo glared at them. Then he said, "*Siete due stronzi!* You are both shitheads!"

Both turned to Angelo and returned looks of alarm.

Angel peered at Paolo and said, "Paolo, you're an unbearable pain in the ass."

Paolo's eyes widened in astonishment.

"And Mauro, you need to have some *coglioni*. Have some balls – the two of you."

"What?" both of them asked simultaneously.

"Yes – you both need to have some balls. Get over yourselves."

Paolo shook his head. Mauro feared Angelo would reveal his secret and glared at him, hoping to dissuade the disclosure.

"*Senta* – listen. Paolo, this is a beautiful piece of land, and you are a fool for letting it go. I apologize for what I am about to say, but I will say it anyway. Your parents will be gone in a year or two. Don't let the opportunity for real love pass you by because you feel some kind of guilt or obligation to remain at their side. They want you to be happy. Look at this man," he said, pointing to Mauro. "He's in love with you. He always has been. He's a catch – handsome, accomplished, and eligible. Mauro. Yes, Paolo is clueless and says things that are hurtful, but deep down, he's in love with you. He needs a push. A big push."

Angelo raised his brows, looked at Mauro, and nodded encouragingly. "Go on!"

Mauro shook his head no.

Angelo glared at him, daring him.

Mauro began to walk away. Angelo took hold of his elbow and pulled him back. "No. You need to do this!"

Mauro shook his head.

Angelo gave him a nod.

Paolo looked confused.

Timidly, Mauro turned to Paolo and said, "Paolo, I would like to." He stopped mid-sentence and shook his head, turning toward Angelo. "*Non posso.* I can't."

"Yes, you can."

Mauro took a deep breath and said, "Paolo. The other day, Angelo said there was a buyer for the vineyard. Well . . . uh . . . it was me."

"You?"

"Yes. I spoke with Angelo about buying the vineyard. I hoped it might be a way for us to move forward, to create something together. I knew you couldn't maintain it on your own, and I needed to sell my home in Rome. I can't stay there anymore. The memories are too unsettling."

"But?"

"When we talked the other day, you didn't seem like you wanted to fight for us, to find a way to make it work. You seemed only mildly interested in maintaining a connection."

"*Uno stronzo,*" Angelo reiterated. "As I said before, he's a shithead."

"I withdrew my offer."

"But I couldn't have you buy the property like that."

"Why not?"

Paolo hesitated. He could feel his chest constrict, and tears formed in his eyes. "I'm not worth it."

"What do you mean?"

"Just what I said. You'd be spending a lot of money, making a big investment. What if it doesn't work out? What if I'm a big disappointment?"

"I'm not buying you. It's an investment in us, in a link that endured, remarkably, over the years. It would be a fitting tribute to Carlo – the dream of redeeming himself and his Italian heritage."

Paolo began to sob. "*Non lo merito. Non sono degno* – I'm not worthy. I'm a mess."

Angelo nodded to Mauro and walked away to give them space. Mauro placed his arm around Paolo. Frank, Sophia, and the others looked on from a distance.

"I know what you feel. I felt it for countless years with Anna. If we try to love in a way that dishonors our true feelings, we will fall short, and we will feel inadequate. It's disempowering and breeds anger, resentment, and apathy. Both of us carry the scars of that. Both of us feel like we are not enough, that we've let others down. It's time for us to follow our hearts."

"But I'm afraid."

"Me too. I'm not sure I can put up with your moodiness."

Paolo chuckled and wiped a tear from his eye. "What do I do about my parents and work?"

"We'll figure that out. I've always wanted to visit Boston. Maybe we commute."

"And you want to sell your place in Rome?"

Mauro nodded.

"Do you have any intolerable idiosyncrasies? I've been on my own for quite a while."

Mauro looked off pensively. "Let me see," he began. "Nope. I don't have any."

"Conceit becomes you," Paolo said, grinning.

"It's a big house and a lot of land. We can give each other space."

"Wait until you see my condo in Boston."

"Maybe Frank can give me an office at the university."

Paolo's eyes widened. He realized the idea of Mauro teaching in the US wasn't farfetched. It might just be an interesting arrangement.

"Shall we?"

"Shall we what?"

"Go sign some papers at Angelo's?"

Both looked over at Angelo, who was having a conversation with Frank. He sensed he was being observed and glanced up. They both nodded, and Angelo smiled.

20

Chapter Twenty – One Year Later

One Year Later

Mauro heard the baby make a few cries and a whimper. He hoped she would fall asleep. Emilia and her husband, Lorenzo, had gone to town for supplies. Mauro agreed to watch Anna.

Paolo strolled in from outside. He was dusty and leaned toward Mauro to give him a kiss. Mauro pressed his hand against his chest in protest. "You need to wash up!"

"It's hard work making wine," Paolo said in self-defense.

"How's it going?"

"Sophia's got everything under control. David is helping. They have finished crushing the first truckload."

"I'm so glad she agreed to help again," Mauro remarked.

"Frank wasn't crazy about the idea. I think they have an active excavation site outside of Naples."

"Ah, yes. Those pesky archaeological projects."

"By the way, when do you have to go to Sicily for your next site visit?"

"In a couple of weeks. Do you want to come too?"

"I don't think your colleagues are crazy about my hanging around."

"Hmm, yes. They're trying to get used to the idea of us."

"I'll be okay here. There's a lot to do in monitoring the fermentation."

"How long will Sophia be around?"

"Another couple of days. She will travel back and forth to Naples."

"And Gino?" Mauro asked with a raised brow.

"Under control."

"Are you sure?"

Paolo nodded. "He and Nico seem to be hitting it off nicely."

"Nico's a schoolteacher in Frascati, right? A bit older."

"You know Gino and his taste for more mature men!"

"I know to keep my eyes on him when the two of you are working together," Mauro noted.

"I give him no encouragement."

"He doesn't need any."

They both laughed.

Paolo went back to the bathroom to clean up. He passed the credenza in the living room filled with photos of Carlo and Luisa, Enzo and Rita, and several pictures he had retrieved from the shoebox, blowing them up and putting them in frames. There was the large gathering of young people from 1995, and his favorite, the one of Mauro and him, arm in arm. He smiled and continued to the back of the house.

He undressed and walked into the bathroom. Glancing at his physique in the mirror, he breathed a sigh of relief. The exercise and weightlifting were paying off. His waist was thin again, and his chest had some definition. He realized that if he could just cut back on the pasta, he would be fine. "But I'm in Italy," he murmured to himself. "You're in fucking Italy," he said with more inflection, making a face in the mirror. He looked up and said, "Carlo, you'd be proud of me now!"

"Of course, he's proud of you. Always was," Mauro said, standing in the doorway, listening in.

"Shit! You scared the hell out of me," Paolo said in shock as he turned around.

"Looking good, old man."

"*Vai via.* I have to clean up."

"Can't I watch?"

"No. You have a baby to watch."

"She's asleep."

"She might wake."

"We're all alone for a few minutes," Mauro said seductively.

"I never knew kids were so much work!" Paolo remarked, approaching Mauro and running his hand over his shoulder.

"Nor boyfriends."

"I resemble that," Paolo said, giving Mauro a warm kiss.

"Can you believe it? A year?" Mauro asked, stroking Paolo's chest.

"We have old lady Angelo to thank for that," Paolo noted.

"Isn't he coming over for dinner tomorrow? You're making Luisa's sauce, right?"

"Sunday gravy, as they call it in Boston."

"I still don't get that."

"Me neither."

"Nor the whole thing about meatballs."

"It's an American touch."

"I like it. I always had fantasies about America."

"And how did they turn out?"

"Better than the dreams."

"Ahh," Paolo said. "Now go watch Anna. I have to shower."

Mauro nodded and retreated. Paolo showered and returned to the kitchen with a fresh pair of shorts and a pullover. "I'm going to check on Sophia. See if she needs any help."

"I'll stay here and watch Anna while her mother and father are out running errands."

Paolo left the back of the house and strolled up the hill and over the ridge to the new barn, cellar, and greenhouse. He walked inside and saw Sophia hard at work.

"Sophia, do you need some help with that?" Paolo asked as he observed her turning on the crusher.

"No, thanks. But if you can bring the next wagonload in, that would be great."

Paolo nodded. He walked toward Sophia and asked, "So, how do they look?"

"Excellent. Same as last year."

"That vintage has proven extraordinary. Everyone in the area is asking about the new American vintner."

"That's you they are asking about," Sophia said to Paolo.

"No. They know there's a sleuth winemaker behind the operation, and they are all jealous."

She chuckled and watched the grapes enter the machine.

Paolo walked outside and leaped onto the tractor. It was Carlo's old machine. Mauro had given it a fresh coat of paint. He turned on the ignition and slowly moved it toward the cellar. "I'll leave it here," he said to Sophia. "I am going to prep the barrels. I know it's still a while before they are to be filled, but I want everything to be ready."

She nodded.

Paolo walked toward the back of the cellar. He loved the tranquility of the space, the special glow of the antique lights, the cool air, and the promise of delicious wine. The barrels had been wet stored and needed to be emptied and then steam rinsed. Mauro had connected piping and pumps so that the barrels didn't have to be rolled outside.

He gazed with pride at the racks of wine from last year's *vendemmia*. He brushed dust off the top row and used a broom to sweep the stone pavement. As he shifted his weight, he felt one of the stones wobble. "Hmm," he said to himself. "I should get some sand to level that."

He used a crowbar to lift the stone so that he could throw some sand underneath. To his surprise, there was a discolored subsurface. His heart began to pound. He used some water to rinse it. The bright colors of the ancient tesserae glistened in the light. "*Cazzo*," he exclaimed in alarm at the mosaic underneath. He quickly threw sand on the tiles and laid the heavy stone back on top. He rinsed his hands in the hose and walked swiftly to the front of the cellar. Mauro was there. He had brought a platter with sandwiches, fruit, and chips.

"*Tesoro*, here's your lunch."

"Aren't we going to eat with Emilia when she's back?" Paolo asked, his heart racing in reaction to the discovery he had just made and had covered over.

"She and Lorenzo had something in town."

"It's nice having them here," Paolo remarked.

"Hmm, yes. It means a lot to me. It is a way to preserve the fond memories I have of my wife. I'm so glad Emilia and Lorenzo named their daughter Anna."

"Emilia misses her. She laments that her mother never met her granddaughter," Paolo said thoughtfully.

"I have a feeling Anna is still around, looking over her family."

"You're getting metaphysical on me. This is a side of the Paolo Minetti I never knew existed," Mauro noted.

"It's funny. When I came back to sell the property, I could swear Carlo and Luisa were around. Periodically, I smelled Carlo's cigarettes or Luisa's perfume. There were too many curious things that happened, not the least of which was meeting you."

Mauro smiled contently.

Paolo's eyes teared up.

"Are you okay?"

"I miss my parents. I miss my grandparents. I feel so adrift."

"It can't be easy when your last family member passes," Mauro said, reaching his arms around Paolo.

Paolo looked out over the field of vines and felt the security of Mauro's embrace. He knew Carlo, Luisa, Enzo, and Rita had loved him, and he had made peace with them in the end. He grew to appreciate that his sense of isolation and aloneness wasn't a defect in him, but a defense he erected around his heart. Mauro tore those defenses down and inspired him to trust and love. He was at home at last, in Italy – where the earth held secrets, where the sun warmed the heart, and where the vines produced their tonic.

Author

Author

Michael Hartwig is a Boston and Provincetown-based author of LGBTQ+ fiction. Hartwig is an accomplished professor of religion and ethics as well as an established artist.

Hartwig grew up in Dallas but spread his wings early on – living in Rome for five years, moving to New England later, and then working in the area of educational travel to the Middle East and Europe. His fiction weaves together his interest in LGBTQ+ studies, ethics, religion, art, languages, and travel. The books are set in international venues. They include rich local descriptions and are peppered with the local language. Characters grapple not only with their own gender and sexuality but with prevailing paradigms of sexuality and family in the world around them.

Hartwig has a facility for fast-paced plots that transport readers to other worlds. They are romantic and steamy as well as thoughtful and engaging. Hartwig imagines rich characters who are at crossroads in their lives. In many instances, these crossroads mirror cultural ones. There's plenty of sexual tension to keep readers on the edge of their seats, but the stories are enriched by broader considerations – historical, cultural, and philosophical.

Other Titles:
Crossing Borders

Old Vines
Entwined
First Crush
Oliver and Henry
A Roman Spell
Love Unearthed
Our Roman Pasts
A Collision in Quebec
Don't Push Me
Transito Seville
The Accidental Italian

For more information on published and forthcoming books visit:

www.michaelhartwigauthor.com